HADES

SPEED DATING WITH THE DENIZENS OF THE UNDERWORLD

BOOK FOURTEEN

ARIEL DAWN

NAUGHTY NIGHTS PRESS LLC • CANADA

HADES

Love is a special kind of Hell...

There are some things Hades can count on in this afterlife—but love isn't one of them.

When he finds himself at a speed dating event at the DeLux Cafe, he discovers a

HADES

connection that will test every ounce of his hard-won self-control.

Too bad the object of his desires happens to be Hecate's best friend, and they are all in the middle of a supernatural mess...

As the lines blur between fate and temptation, can Hades rise above his own demons? Or will history repeat itself—and bring him to his knees?

Hades is book fourteen in the Speed Dating with the Denizens of the Underworld shared world, filled with fiery gods, feisty heroines, ride or die besties, and romance that will leave you begging for more!

CHAPTER ONE

HADES SAT AT the bar in the DeLux Cafe, swirling his Manhattan.

It wasn't as if he hated social events, in fact, it was the opposite. He craved social interaction. Spending a multitude of years in the depths of the Underworld tended to have that effect, but it was home.

Work came first. It always came first.

HADES

Souls needed to be ferried and sorted. Quotas needed to be met, lest he wished to obtain a visit from Lucifer, his employer.

CEO of Hell just didn't have the same ring as the devil himself.

But even Hades knew that too much work and no play would make him a dull god, and so he'd agreed to step out of his dark and gloomy cave and partake in the surface happenings at least a few times a year. Four to be exact.

One outing per season.

He dreaded this time of year though, the fall.

After all, it meant winter was near.

And every winter he thought of her.

Persephone... Hades hated how his thoughts traveled to her. The life they'd had when they were young.

Well, younger, really.

I've been young my whole life.

It didn't help that tales of their forbidden romance were still written over and over again in books, movies, and songs. There was even a comic he could read on his phone, which featured their love rather prominently.

He actually kind of liked Lore Olympus, if he was being honest. The artwork was so colorful and despite being a creature that existed in the darkness... he loved colorful.

She didn't even remember him, though, not anymore.

Not since she'd been kidnapped, and her memory erased.

Since it was discovered Hell was literally killing her.

Hades took another sip of his

HADES

Manhattan, hoping it would quiet his solemn thoughts.

He'd known the right thing to do at the time, but it wasn't easy.

But had Persephone stayed in Hell—she would have withered away in a slow, beautiful death.

Death was not what he wished for her, no. He wished for life.

Persephone's only chance at life was to be without him. To be freed from the chains of Hell he'd instilled on her.

So, he let her go.

A shoulder brushed his, bringing him out of his thoughts, and he looked up from his drink momentarily to see a short brunette with bright blue eyes leaning languidly over the counter, batting her eyelashes at the bartender.

His gaze roved down the curve of her spine, resting on a rather round, plump behind. The sight elicited thoughts almost instinctively, and he had to grasp his drink to still the itch in his palm.

The itch to feel flesh beneath it, to deliver a sting that would make such a beautiful mortal whimper in his grasp.

Do not get so excited so quickly, this damn thing hasn't even begun yet!

He chastised himself before he turned his attention back to his drink and away from the ass in question.

"Hades, how you been, man?" The familiar voice of a rather annoying hunter broke his concentration.

Orion.

Great.

Is there anywhere this pain in the ass

does not go?

"Hello, Orion," Hades responded politely.

The blond-haired hunter took the open seat next to Hades, never asking if the seat was taken. It was bad enough Hades had to reside near the man in the Underworld, not to mention due to Orion's contracts with both Heaven and Hell, he was a frequent flier in the offices Hades worked.

"Haven't seen you in a while, work must be Hell," Orion said as he nodded at the bartender, signaling a drink order.

Hades sipped his Manhattan again, contemplating leaving the bar altogether. It would be so much easier to just take a trip over to the Den Of Sin than to go through all the motions of speed dating. He could easily move up his appointment with

Tenille or give Samael and his bouncers a momentary scramble if he showed up unannounced, which could prove to be entertaining. Though, he did enjoy the idea of engaging in the pursuit, the challenge, and also the fantasy that perhaps maybe he would find someone in the sea of hopeless romantics and lonely singles who would stir his interest in ways that didn't end with an empty bed come morning.

Hades mocked Orion with a sarcastic laugh. "Don't quit your day job, Orion."

"Wasn't planning on it." Orion took a swig of his beer.

Hades despised beer. It hadn't changed much over the centuries and still tasted as dull as the day it was created. He preferred well aged wine and scotch, the kind that was only available to a select few, followed only by his love of an expertly crafted Manhattan. The bartender at the DeLux was not an expert by any means, but the drink would suffice, nonetheless.

"Work's been kind of a downer lately," the persistent man droned on.

"I left the confines of Hell to escape, Orion. I do not wish to speak of—"

"I mean, I guess things are slow everywhere, really, I've heard the angels aren't faring any better." Orion shrugged.

Hades grasped his glass tighter. Before Hades could get up and dislodge himself from Orion's titillating watercooler conversation, a savior with dark hair and dual-colored eyes came to scare off the hunter.

"Cate!" Hades's voice raised several octaves. He was rather surprised to see his friend. After all, she did not enjoy social gatherings quite as much as he did.

Orion nearly fell off his chair as Hades stood up and pulled the goddess into a friendly embrace.

"Hades." Cate's lips turned up in a small smile as she returned his embrace before leaning on the bar languidly, her dark raven locks falling over her exposed shoulders.

Orion stuttered, nearly spitting out his beer.

"Cate... you're looking—"

Cate flashed Orion a look that made her dual-toned eyes glow, a menacing look that Hades could only smile at.

"It's Hecate to you, hunter," she said cooly.

"Uh—" he stammered as Hades let out a

chuckle. As if perfectly on cue, a tall blonde passed their proximity, heading toward the tables lit with tiny candles, readying herself for the oncoming speed dating, and Orion was enticed far too easily.

"Catch up with you two later," Orion said as he took off in the direction of the blonde gazelle.

"I thought you'd sworn off dating," Hades said with amusement as Hecate—or as she liked to be called nowadays, Cate—ordered her drink. Some pomegranate apple concoction that was the house special this evening.

"Who says I'm looking for a date?" she asked, crossing her arms as she let her gaze rove over the crowd.

Hades shook his head, a smile curving

on his lips. "Cate. It's speed dating. It's in the name. You don't have to lie, we all get lonely..."

"I'm perfectly fine on my own. I do not get lonely," she retorted to him, eyes scanning the crowd still.

He knew better than to press her. Just the fact she had left her cabin and joined the world of the living was enough of a feat in itself and he did not wish to give her reason to retreat.

"Of course not," he said, his voice thick with sarcasm. "How is Spike, by the way?" Hades took a sip of his drink and Cate's entire demeanor shifted.

There was nothing the goddess of the moon loved more than animals. She spent most of her time away from her cabin on the edge of the forest managing and running the New Haven Animal Rescue, tending to all sorts of animals.

Which was why when Spike, one of the hellhounds in his department's care, had become injured, he had no question in the world who to call. Yet, he should have known the moment she had to keep him for longer than a week that he was going to be short a hellhound and would have to fudge the paperwork somewhere.

Which he gladly did without question, knowing Spike was in hellhound heaven under the care of the goddess Hecate.

Cate's eyes sparkled with affection as she smiled back at him. "Oh, he's just the best!" she exclaimed.

Hades lifted his glass to her before finishing the last of his drink, glad to hear the arrangement had worked out.

The bartender approached with his refill and Cate's pomegranate apple cocktail. She opened her hand purse, which was a vinyl clutch in the shape of a skull, fingering around for cash before Hades stopped her by placing a hand over hers.

"I got this."

True to her nature, she rolled her eyes and huffed indignantly. "I can buy my own drink."

"I know you can, but we are friends, are we not?" He did his best to look at her pleadingly, but could not help smiling. Her shoulders eased only a fraction and she twisted her lips, clearly debating how to answer. But Hades did not give her the chance to protest. "You deserve to have a little fun. So, please, stow your bitchcraft—"

"My what?" Cate's voice raised an

octave, and a faint wind carried in the space between them, blowing strands of her ebony hair about lightly.

She was rather easy to rile up after all, but then again she was out of her element. Out of her comfort zone. He only hoped that this would be a pleasurable experience for her. It had been years since she'd openly engaged in any sort of romantic endeavors, even if they were only endeavors that involved her magic.

"You are so much fun to rattle, and so easy." He smirked at her. "Let loose, Cate. Forget about all your troubles and have some fucking fun."

He couldn't even remember the last man or woman she'd been with, let alone someone she felt close enough to to open herself up again. She was convinced no one could love her, convinced if somehow they could, that she would wind up hurt.

He expected a sharp comeback, but all she said was, "Thanks for the drink."

Hades raised his glass in return, smirking at her once more. He took a sip of his fresh Manhattan as Cate scurried off toward the open seating, readying for the onslaught of daters about to commence, figuring now would be as good a time as ever to do the same.

CHAPTER TWO

DARCY'S HEAD ONLY felt slightly hazy, which she blamed on the alcohol rather than the vampire she was straddling in the booth on the opposite side of the bar.

Though vampires tended to be able to wield mind tricks like a Jedi master, for some reason, Darcy was immune to their tactics. But, she was not immune to their sex appeal.

There's just something about being that close to danger, that close to dancing with death...

Though, it seemed out of all the supernaturals she could have selected tonight, she'd placed her bets on a newborn vampire who didn't seem to know his way around a woman almost as much as he didn't know how to use his fangs.

Or perhaps, he's just afraid...

When the vampire, whose name she did not bother to learn, broke away from his attention on her neck, Darcy felt a gentle gust of wind pass her.

She'd only known one person who had that effect. Her friend, Cate, or as she was known in ancient fables, the goddess Hecate.

Darcy pushed the nameless vampire back as she dislodged herself from his lap.

"Is something wrong?" he asked, his voice slightly off-kilter, probably from the euphoria of being so close to her blood while heavily aroused.

It didn't take much to seduce a vampire, just the promise of sex and blood. The idea of it was enough to get their juices flowing. Even the awkward ones.

"I, ummm, I'm sorry this has been fun and all, but I think my ride's leaving..."

The vampire actually had the audacity to look hurt.

Darcy sighed as she grabbed her phone from the table once more, sliding it into her pocket as she hurriedly made her exit.

"Do you want my number?" he called out above the chatter, and Darcy cringed at the desperation in his voice.

Maybe I need to switch to shifters instead...

Darcy let her thoughts wander to the gossip she pretended not to notice in the breakroom, the whispers of her co-workers from the New Haven Animal Rescue.

Apparently, shifters did it better according to them, what with coexisting with literal animals as part of their DNA and all. She had heard they were also genuinely more confident, especially the alphas.

I've never been with an alpha male of any kind...

Just as her thoughts started to drift off on a tangent once more, Darcy caught sight of Cate with another man, a man in a fine suit to be exact—who was carrying an unconscious man in his arms, a look of utter amusement on his face as Cate walked hurriedly in the direction of the New Haven Animal Rescue van.

What the hell is she doing?

Darcy's interest was piqued rather easily, truth be told. She'd always had quite the penchant for sticking her nose in where it didn't belong, for snooping, and for finding herself in the middle of situations one should not be a part of.

Which was exactly why she followed Cate and her mystery men without question.

She'd been friends with the goddess ever since she was a small child, and she wagered there was not anyone on this plane who knew Cate Moon as well as she. It had taken her much convincing to even get the woman to agree to come to the DeLux Cafe's speed dating event in the first place, and she was not about to let her friend walk away without explaining herself.

"Leaving so soon?" Darcy said with amusement as she crossed her arms upon reaching the van. She could see Cate was rather panic-stricken.

True to her nature, Cate brushed her off. "I don't have time to explain."

"Of course you don't." Darcy rolled her eyes. So predictable.

The man in the suit looked between Cate and Darcy, his gaze settling on her for a moment too long to be considered polite, and in that moment Darcy felt a lightbulb go off in her brain.

No wonder he looks familiar, she

thought as memory served her correctly.

He's the guy from the bar! The one who was checking out my ass...

Darcy fought a maddening blush at the memory and was about to persist with Cate, but the man spoke before she could find a chance.

His voice was dark, haunting even, yet, it carried an air of sophistication in its tone.

"Cate, who is this mortal that dares to challenge you?" the hot man in the suit said almost too perfectly.

Shit, this man could sell me ice with that voice if I lived in the arctic...

Cate sighed as she threw open the back doors of the van, not bothering to look at Darcy or the hottie in the suit with the nice voice.

"Hades, meet Darcy. Darcy, meet Hades," Cate said as if she was doing nothing more than delivering the weather.

Darcy's eyes widened at the name. There was no way...

She knew Cate had a past before she came to the woods, before she'd left the supernatural societies abundant both above and below Earth, but she didn't talk about such things often, if at all. The life she'd lived before humanity forced her on the edges of civilization. But as she spoke the introductions and rounded her way to the driver's side of the van, Darcy gazed at the man Cate called Hades. She took in his fine suit, his dark hair swept back casually, not a hair out of place. His dark, almost black eyes.

"Hades? Like, God of the Underworld,

Hades?" she asked, her voice hitching in surprise.

"It appears my reputation precedes me," Hades said with a smile that showcased teeth so perfect and white he could have been in a toothpaste ad. His voice was smooth and decadent, and combined with the fancy suit and that smile...

"Cate, you didn't tell me—" Darcy started as she scurried to the passenger side of the van, not wasting a moment as she jumped in just as she heard the back doors slamming shut.

"There's a lot of things I've never divulged, Darcy. Don't take it personally," Cate said while starting the car. Darcy noted as she turned the keys in the ignition that her hand shook. She took a moment to look over her shoulder, fastening herself into her seat, knowing Cate's driving was more of a roller coaster ride than an actual roller coaster. Hades sat in the back of the van with the unconscious man lying on the floor, his head in Hades's lap. He looked positively lifeless.

Dead, even.

"What's with the dead guy?" Darcy questioned aloud, although she was not certain who she was asking. Nevertheless, Hades answered her with that smooth, decadent voice of his.

"He isn't dead. I would know," Hades said definitively.

Darcy found her lips turning up in a smile, most intrigued by the god of death riding in the back of her work van. "Is he always this fun at parties?" she asked lightly as Cate backed the vehicle up rather abruptly.

"Darcy..." Her friend's tone carried a hint of warning, and any other mortal, perhaps, would be frightened. But Cate threatened Darcy on an almost daily basis, and the last fifteen years in the presence of the goddess made Darcy realize that most of the time, when it came to their friendship—Cate's bark was worse than her bite.

"Is this why you don't want to come out? Get you around a good time, some drinks and hot guys and you turn all serial killer?" she prodded.

"He's not dead!" Hades's voice rose in annoyance, and Darcy noted the hint of panic hidden within it as well.

Why on Earth would he be panicking

over a dead—not dead—guy?

Isn't this like normal for him?

"I wasn't trying to hurt him, really. I just wanted to give him back his stupid rock, maybe give his drunk ass a ride home..." Cate started to ramble in her own frustration. Darcy couldn't help but poke the anxious goddess, knowing that now was the best time to keep her going. She was far more likely to divulge secrets when in the throes of rambling such as this.

That was how Darcy found out about the crush Cate had had on one of the vet techs a few years back. She'd encouraged her friend to pursue her feelings, but Cate only kept them to herself, wanting to be professional.

"I didn't peg you for the type to take advantage of a hot drunk guy but—"

"Oh my word, Darcy! That is not what I was doing!" Cate retorted with exasperation.

"In the olden days, men used to throw themselves at her feet," Hades chimed in from the back, a soft chuckle escaping his lips. Darcy couldn't help but turn around, seeing that show stopping smile once more. The sight alone—the god of the Underworld... smiling... was a sight that was both intriguing and also strangely alluring. "No alcohol needed. Just pure, unfiltered sex magick."

Darcy giggled as she turned her gaze back to her friend, who looked to be turning six shades of red.

"Hades!" She scolded the god as if he were nothing more than a petulant child, but he only had the audacity to laugh at her.

I could get used to this guy, that's for sure!

Glad to know I'm not the only one who can push her buttons.

"I knew it! It's always the quiet ones," she teased Cate, feeling emblazoned by Hades's banter toward her friend.

"Don't listen to him. His memory is shaded by the fact he hides in a fucking dungeon all day with the undead," Cate snapped, and Darcy couldn't help her giggling turning into an all out laugh at her frazzled demeanor.

She'd never seen Cate like this, and quite frankly, she didn't dislike it.

"So, did he pass out before you made your move or—" she continued to pry.

"Oh, for the love..." Cate huffed at them

both as she slammed on the brakes; the motion jostling the car. Bottles and supplies crashed to the ground with a thud and Hades lurched forth with the unconscious man, nearly hitting the edge of Darcy's seat with the back of his head. Hades groaned as she whined, their protests filling the air.

"You didn't have to come with me," Cate said in a calmer voice.

"I would be loath to refrain from following a situation that may result in death," Hades said poignantly. Darcy watched as Cate rolled her eyes before speaking.

"You think I'm going to let you walk away from speed dating with an unconscious man who looks like that... without getting all the details?" she answered, playfully shoving Cate's arm. Her friend let out a deep sigh.

"Hades..." Cate called out, turning only for a moment in his direction. Darcy watched their interaction, watched as he looked up at her as if waiting for her command.

How interesting...

"Yes, Cate?" His voice was so clear and crisp that her skin prickled with goosebumps.

"Can you use your magic to sense other energies? Energies that aren't... alive?" Cate spoke cautiously, and Darcy wondered why all of a sudden her friend's tone had shifted. It was as if she wasn't saying something, and that intrigued Darcy like a moth to a flame.

"You mean spiritual energy? Yes, why?"

he answered her solidly.

"I feel an energy coming off of him... but I can't figure out what it is."

Darcy knew Cate could feel energy. It was one of the reasons she often liked to cite when refusing to leave her cabin, though Darcy never gave up trying to convince her to do so. Part of her godly DNA was being able to sense energies, both the good and bad. She'd claimed that being around people was overwhelming because of the abundance of energies that surrounded them, and, up until this moment, Darcy had thought it was all some made up excuse.

She watched Hades and Cate exchange looks, listened to them talk back and forth about a crystal and magic. About energies. She watched Hades's hands hover above the man in the backseat, smokey blue energy radiating from his fingertips... and she knew Cate had been telling the truth. But the thought made her wonder still.

Could all gods read energy like that?

Or, was it just a trick that worked purely on mortals?

Cate's bone-chilling scream jostled her from her thoughts, as a resounding "Fuck!" rattled in the space between them all. As if perfectly on cue, the van clunked and hissed before stopping altogether.

Darcy closed her eyes and took a deep breath.

We really need to get the van looked at again...

"It's okay, Cate, just breathe..." Darcy said calmly, knowing there was nothing that aggravated Cate more than the fickleness of their van.

"I am breathing!" she yelled back, clearly feeling the strain of the evening's events.

Hades must have been familiar with such outbursts, for he leapt into action as well, his smooth voice taking on an almost hypnotic tone.

"I would suggest..." he started, but Cate did not let him finish.

"I did not ask your opinion. I did not ask you to come with me in this stupid, dilapidated, piece of shit van!" she said as she smacked her hand on the steering wheel in a small burst of rage. Something in the back fell off a shelf, the sound of it clattering against the floor almost comical.

"It's not like it's the first time you've broken down," Darcy reminded her. It was the truth. They'd spent more than their fair share of time calling AAA or when Darcy had been dating Roger, the mechanic…

Cate looked at Hades in question. "Do you know how to fix a broken down van?" she asked almost pleadingly.

The sight alone would have been funny if they were not in the middle of the road at this hour.

"Do I look like I dabble in automotive engineering?" he huffed.

"Hades…" Cate growled once more, tapping her long, black, coffin-shaped nails against the steering wheel. A sure sign her patience was wearing thin.

"Perhaps, you should look for help," Darcy prodded, unable to leave well enough alone.

"And where, pray tell, am I going to find

help at one o'clock in the morning on a shitty road on the outskirts of town?" she purred, her voice rather alluring... but Darcy knew the venom it was holding back. Before Darcy could speak, Hades answered her.

"Perhaps, you should do as the mortals do and find a gas station," Hades said all too seriously, as if he'd only read about such things or seen such scenarios in movies rather than enacted them himself.

Then again, Cate did say he lived in the Underworld... doubt they have cars down there...

"Unbelievable," Cate huffed as she threw open the driver's side door and exited the van with haste.

She slammed the door shut, taking off in the opposite direction, leaving Darcy and

HADES

the god of the Underworld alone with Cate's unconscious date.

CHAPTER THREE

WHAT AM I doing here?

Hades ran over the shocking turn of events in his head, still uncertain how one thing truly led to another. One moment he was sipping his Manhattan, casually flirting with the singles in the room every minute or so, and the next he was following a strange pull of energy. He felt the slight vibration, heard the hum like one could hear electricity surging through wires if they listened hard enough. But even without its sound, he could feel the energy like a living, breathing thing. So, he followed it through the crowd, past the restrooms, and out the door to the alley only to find Cate, of all people, hovering over an unconscious man, sparking in the moonlight, the hum and draw of the unknown energy all around them. The look on her face was one he hadn't seen in eons.

Panic.

So, he leapt into action, assessing the situation. The last thing he wanted was to answer for a death on the premises of the DeLux Cafe. Not only would it be bad for Eve and Aphrodite, but Demi and Hera would certainly not be happy about having to run godly damage control. They were always touting about not drawing undue attention to oneself. That, as gods, they needed to rise above the stereotypical ideals mortals assumed of them—full of themselves, stocked with rage, and easy to anger, powerful killing machines who looked down upon mortals as nothing. Not to mention there was the matter of them being hell-bent on running an "upscale" establishment, such as the DeLux Cafe completely above board. This meant deaths on the premises or anywhere near it were a no-no, and Hades did have a well deserved reputation that wherever he went, death followed, even if nowadays that was not the case. He'd certainly earned it in those days after Persephone had left...

Though it was not his fault that mortals

held the stereotypes they did. Popular literature and the legends that stood the test of time were mostly to blame. The grandeur of these delusions was just simply not true, not in the slightest, but that did not matter. A goddess like Cate, one with a long list of victims as well as a list of those saved—well, if anyone were to get wind the goddess of witchcraft, the moon, and the Keeper of the Wolves was anywhere NEAR something that remotely smelled like death, there would be hell to pay.

And she just got out of the cabin for once...

"So, you and Cate..." Darcy's voice broke his train of thought, bringing him back to the present, and to the unconscious man in his lap. Hades adjusted himself and Gunner—the man did have a name he recalled from checking his wallet earlier—in the back of the van, careful not to upturn the supplies left stable on the wire racks.

Hades looked toward the front to see Darcy had unbuckled her seatbelt, and she was now leaning over the seat rather loosely, hair falling over her shoulder casting a shadow on her soft features. He noticed the curve of her round breasts pushed together, cleavage all but spilling out from her turned position, and he forced his eyes to meet hers.

"I beg your pardon?" He cleared his throat, realizing perhaps he'd been staring at her breasts and her delicious pout far too long.

Perhaps, I should move my appointment

with Tenille up a day…

"You and Cate. What's the story there?" Darcy asked once more and Hades could see the curiosity lit up in her eyes.

If it is gossip you want, my darling, I am afraid you will be sorely disappointed.

"Not much of a story to tell, really. We've known each other for a fairly long time. I consider her a good friend." He shrugged, not wanting to get into all the details. He was not sure how much of her past Cate had divulged to her mortal friend, and he did not wish to get an earful from her later if there were things she'd rather keep private.

"I mean, you aren't like some emo ex-boyfriend or anything, are you?" Her voice carried a hint of amusement, and Hades found his shoulders relaxing, if only a fraction.

Of course.

It's always the same assumption.

Centuries haven't changed a thing.

Hades twisted his lips before answering her. He could still feel the strange energy surrounding them, and his focus seemed to be wavering. He blinked once more, breaking eye contact with Darcy before continuing.

"Absolutely not. Cate is not, as you would say, "my type" for one, but also our relationship has always been purely platonic. She's like the sister I should've had instead of the ones I ended up with." He let out a little chuckle.

Darcy narrowed her eyes.

"What is your type, H?" she asked with a smirk. The question left him feeling rather on the spot, and he was not certain what he should say.

He could not very well tell this woman, this friend of Cate's, his desires—the things he needed. He could not very well tell her that up until he'd found himself in the Den Of Sin, he'd only desired one woman, and though he'd appreciated the beauty of both men and women from time to time, he did not have a set of beauty standards to which he was attracted.

No, his type was not something that came from attractiveness and looks. It was something that came from within, a voice who could command him, and take away the things that held power over him. His memories, his heartache. Something that was full of life, full of humor and sarcasm as well as sweetness and love.

"Darcy." He tasted her name on his tongue and the sound of it uttered between them was heavy in the air. Darcy blinked, her mouth opening just the slightest as he continued.

"I do not typecast lovers. If you must know, my type has nothing to do with outward appearance." He said the words easily enough, and it felt a safe response. She could take it however she wished.

But why do I care what she thinks?

The thoughts were baffling to him, and so he pushed forth the conversation in an effort to avoid more questioning from her.

"And what about you, darling? Do you have a predetermined affinity toward someone in particular?" he said with a grin, hoping to throw her off guard or at the very least make her slightly uncomfortable as her question had made him.

Surprisingly, her eyes lit up as she excitedly exclaimed, "Well, for a while there I thought it was vampires, but I think that's kind of fizzled out. I'd say shifters, but I've never actually like, dated, or slept with a shifter so I'd have to do some research first, but—"

Hades found his blood chilling, and a startling feeling overcame him, one he wasn't entirely sure how to process.

One that did not make sense.

For as Darcy rattled on about her attractions, Hades felt a pang of anger, an overwhelming need to put an end to such notions.

But why would he feel this way over a woman who he just met?

It didn't make any sense to him, and thankfully, a familiar voice pulled him from his inspection.

Finally, Cate is back…

Only as she approached, he could smell the potent scent of Underworld—fire and brimstone, to be certain.

A demon was in their presence.

Hades felt the innate desire to protect and awaken inside him. Though he dealt with demons all the time, he did not wish for the doe-eyed brunette in Cate's passenger seat to become more than acquainted with his underlings, no.

But as the scent grew nearer, he recognized that this was no average demon. For when he heard the flapping of wings, felt the prickle of heat upon them, he knew he was right to worry about

Darcy's well-being.

Because the demon Cate had brought back to help was not a demon at all.

He was Cate's pain in the ass ex.

Who also happened to be his boss.

Hades set Gunner's head down gently on the floor before rushing out of the doors of the van, his eyes meeting Lucifer's with surprise, but also with warning.

"Hades, so good to see you." The fallen angel smiled a wicked smile, and Hades nodded in response, a silent understanding between them. He watched as Cate led the devil himself to the front of the van just as Darcy opened the passenger door.

CHAPTER FOUR

THE NIGHT, IT seemed, was full of surprises. Not only had Darcy stumbled upon Cate in a precarious circumstance, she had discovered that her friend of fifteen years also kept company with some very dark, very devilish men.

Although they were not quite men, were they?

HADES

Lucifer, a fallen angel–the King of Hell itself—and the strangely mysterious, yet insanely attractive Hades, god of the Underworld. Not to mention, there was the shifter who was unconscious riding in the back seat with the sexy god of death, who was also quite appealing to the eye.

How many hot supernatural men did Cate know?

Though she suspected, if tonight was any indication, it was probably more than she wanted to disclose.

Hades had mentioned Cate used to partake in sex magick, and though Darcy was not sure what that entailed, she had her ideas.

Well, I guess magic pussy will draw out some finer breed of dick than the rest of us have a shot at.

She'd watched in interest as Lucifer jolted the battery of the van back to life, as Cate gritted her teeth and said 'thank you.' She felt more than curious to know what the story was between the two. So, she made a mental note to ask tomorrow morning when she planned to stop by and check on her friend.

Though Darcy had faith in Cate, that if anyone could bring Gunner out of stasis as Hades had explained, it was probably Cate. Darcy was no stranger to Cate's magical abilities; most of said abilities were applied to daily living situations, such as enchanting her cabin or even using her magic to manipulate the auras of the animals at New Haven during certain difficult procedures.

But, she had seen Cate awaken animals

under deep anesthesia, so she figured a human wouldn't be that much of a stretch.

***

Yet, as she stood on Cate's doorstep next to the finely dressed Hades, she found herself feeling somewhat nervous for her friend. She trusted that whatever needed to be done, would indeed be done, but she also saw the way Cate kept looking at Gunner. Like he was a meal and she was fucking starving.

Perhaps that had something to do with the lines of energy she saw between them. The ones coming from the rock, or the Diviner as Cate and Hades had called it.

She wasn't entirely certain what it meant, and she hadn't had a moment to ask.

The lines appeared vividly when Cate was in Gunner's presence, even with him being unconscious, but they'd also appeared when Cate was nowhere near the van.

When it was just her and Hades. She'd followed their light directly to the center of his chest, and though she'd meant to ask him what they were, if he could see them...

She did not mention it in the slightest. Her instincts told her, for once, to play it by ear. Not to make any sudden movements or accusations.

The two of them sat in the van in open solitude. Darcy held the keys, hovering in the ignition before she finally took a deep breath and started the car.

"So, where do you want me to drop you off at?" she asked as she turned in Hades's direction.

In his fine silk suit, contrasted by nothing more than a deep red tie, he looked positively dashing, but certainly out of place in the van next to her.

Like something out of my wildest dreams...

She focused all her attention on trying to look unaffected. Normal even. The last thing she wanted to do was start rambling again for fear of looking like an overexcited poodle with Tourettes, but then again, she was quite nervous. The only god she'd ever known happened to be one that preferred animals to people, and who she would bet would not look quite as appealing in a suit.

"I will retire after I have seen you home safely," his velveteen voice said matter-of-factly. Darcy's eyes fluttered momentarily as images of a soft, smooth tongue stroked her brain without warning. She blinked, trying to push them away.

Fucking hell... get your shit together, Darcy!

"I... ummm... that's really not necessary, I'm fine," she said with a shrug. Her stomach grumbled loudly, and Hades raised an eyebrow.

"Perhaps we should feed you first." He smirked.

"I mean, I'm not going to say no to food, by any means." She smiled, feeling a shiver of excitement, despite it being two-thirty in the morning.

Hades pulled out a small post-it notepad from his front pocket, studying it closely.

"Ummm, what is that?" Darcy said as

she started to back the van up.

"I come to the surface four times a year. While I'm here, I try to write down the places I'd like to go, places recommended to me mostly but some I find myself."

"And you don't just enter it into your phone like a normal person?" she prodded, focusing her eyesight on the road in front of her. Though they hadn't quite discussed their options, not many places were open at this hour other than Taco Tim's. Taco Tim's also happened to be right next door to her apartment complex.

"Do you like tacos?" Darcy asked, trying to keep her newfound company talking.

Silence always bothered her, but if he was talking, chances were she'd ramble less, and if she rambled less then she would most certainly not look like a crazy person.

Since when have I ever cared about how other people see me?

Hades looked up from his post-it.

"I don't dislike them," he answered mysteriously.

"Well, our only option for grub at this hour is probably Taco Tim's, which has margaritas, so that's my vote," she said as she stopped at a traffic light.

"Nothing good has ever come from a margarita at three in the morning," he said as his lips curved into a delicious smile. Darcy could feel the blush creeping up her neck and she had no choice but to turn away from him. Thankfully, as she did so, the light turned green.

"That depends on your definition of good," she chuckled as the two of them

rode off into the night toward the light of
Taco Tim's.

CHAPTER FIVE

HADES HAD NEVER seen goblets so large for one person. The goblets that the waitress had brought them looked to be the size of goldfish bowls, packed to the brim with crushed ice, and decorated with a heaping amount of salt and sugar.

While Darcy had opted for a strawberry margarita, Hades had kept it simple with a classic margarita.

Darcy stretched her arm out across the table, swooping a large chip into the plastic salsa bowl. The chili pepper lights strewn about on the outside of the food truck lit up the otherwise dark parking lot where Taco Tim's stood, casting a warm glow on Darcy's skin and chocolate brown hair.

Though the hum of the energy surrounding them had diminished once Gunner and Cate had parted ways, Hades still could not shake the feeling that something had changed within him. Like the world around him had suddenly shifted, yet everything was the same.

Wasn't it?

"So, speed dating huh?" Darcy raised an eyebrow at him as she popped a chip in her mouth before taking a long drink through her oversized straw.

"I like to surround myself with life when I visit the surface," he said as he cocked his head to the side.

Was this woman judging him?

How absurd it would be of her to do so, considering she was also at the DeLux Cafe for the event. He'd seen the name tag on her shirt at the bar.

"First time?" She dipped another chip in the salsa, some of it sloshing over the side onto the metal table.

"Not really. You?" He gingerly picked up a chip and waited until the coast was clear before dipping lightly once, then popping the chip in his mouth.

"Kind of? It's been a while since..." Darcy seemed to catch herself and instead of finishing her sentence, she opted for a longer drink of her margarita just as the waitress dropped off their tacos.

"Since what?" he asked while inspecting the fare in front of him before taking a bite. The slow roasted meat nearly fell apart on his tongue, the spices awakening his sinuses.

"I've been going through a bit of a dry spell," she said, and as the words fell off her tongue, her own eyes widened as if she could not believe her own mouth.

She hurriedly tried to recover, obviously embarrassed by her abrupt answer, one in which she did not mean to voice to a stranger such as he was.

"Not like I-haven't-had-sex dry spell, but like..." Her eyes fluttered shut and she pursed her lips, taking a deep breath before continuing quickly. "I mean, I've had sex... just...damn it!" She sighed in exasperation. "What I mean is, it's been a while since my last... relationship," she quickly spoke, taking another drink.

"Nothing to be ashamed of," he reassured her, noting that despite her outburst, the flustered look on her face was quite... cute.

"I mean, I was mostly interested because I heard stories about the kind of... clientele... that frequented the DeLux Cafe. My co-worker, Sandy, said there's like... lots of vampires and shifters, and... I wanted to see it for myself, and..."

Hades looked at her inquisitively, but instead of completing her thought, she focused on her taco. He watched as the crema sauce splattered on the side of her mouth, watched as her tongue flicked out and she licked at it before a sweet moan of delight left her lips.

The sight stirred something within him, and immediately his cock twitched; his brain gesturing up plenty of images of what he'd like her to do with said tongue. He took a long drink of his margarita as well, savoring the cold ice and the sour taste of lime.

"Most humans don't know that there are others. Knowing so would cause a great deal of panic," Hades said as he took another bite of food.

"Well yeah, but like... I work in animal rescue. It's not something we advertise, believe me, Cate keeps a pretty good lid on things, but we've definitely ended up with a shifter or two before. It's not as uncommon as you think. Someone calls in about an injured animal, you know, like an animal well beyond the size of what they should be..." she said with a shrug. "That's how I found out about all this stuff. Well, that and Cate. If we ever get any weird cases or something comes up in the news, she'll usually tell me. 'That wasn't a bear attack, it was a shifter, Darcy'"

Hades let out a small chuckle, nearly choking on the remains of his taco as he listened to Darcy mock—no, imitate the goddess so well. She had Cate's stoic, cold tone down pat.

"There's plenty of mortals who know and like that sort of thing. You just need to know where to find them."

Hades could feel his lips curling into a smirk. "And where would one, who is interested, find them?" He patted his mouth with the paper napkin politely.

Darcy sat for a moment, gazing back at him, twisting her lips in thought.

"A woman never kisses and tells, H," she said with a flirtatious smile and a wink as she finished with her plate and took another drink.

The lights of Taco Tim's flickered, and Hades knew it was their signal that they were closing. He got up swiftly, clearing away the boxes and remaining remnants of salsa, even taking the time to clean the bit that had fallen over the side in Darcy's beeline for the dip.

"Well, it's been fun and all, but I should probably head up." Darcy stood, and though she tried to play it off, he could see the falter in her step as she did so.

The energy that emanated off of her was

not intoxicating by any means, but he could sense her emotion tied to it.

Nervousness.

Excitement.

Intrigue.

"May I assist you, darling?" he asked, casually sliding his hands in his pockets. Though he felt anything but casual at the moment, he could not afford to let anyone see his nerves, his anxieties. No, no one would have that luxury ever again.

"I mean, who am I to say no to a god?" she teased. Hades only smirked in response as he strode closer to her.

In seconds, he was within her proximity, close enough he could reach out and touch her, run his finger along her skin, which he noted had goosebumps. Her bright blue eyes gazed up at him, and her lips smiled wickedly.

"Good girl. Now, give me your hand," he said smoothly.

Darcy did not fight his request as she laid her hand in his palm. The touch sent a shockwave through Hades's body, lighting up his nerves and heating his blood, catching him off guard. Yet, he managed to close his hand around hers, focusing on the slightly clammy yet smooth feel of her against him, and then the lights of Taco Tim's went out, and Hades transported the two of them directly to Darcy's doorstep in a matter of seconds.

CHAPTER SIX

DARCY FELT A sudden rush of air all around her, and within seconds she was in front of her apartment door. She had the startling feeling as if the room was spinning, though everything looked to be in place, like every nerve in her body was alert in a way that was most unfamiliar.

She blinked furiously, adjusting to the

light of the hallway, which seemed much brighter suddenly. "What... the..." She tried to find her voice, tried to find her words but she seemed to be at a loss for the moment.

"A god never kisses and tells, darling Darcy." Darcy watched Hades's eyes light up as he smirked at her.

All at once, gravity rushed her, the heat of his gaze stirring up butterflies in her slightly woozy stomach, and Darcy lost her footing, stumbling forward toward the door.

Before she could catch herself, Hades reached out, bracing his arms around her, his right hand sliding around her waist as his left steadied her.

Though she knew she should feel more than mortified—after all, she'd barely been able to hold herself together since she'd stumbled upon him—as she looked up at the god of the Underworld, she felt awakened. As if she had finally found the confidence she'd been looking for all evening.

I'm sure the margarita is to blame, too.

Dark brown eyes stared back at her and it was as if they could see through all of her. Past her skin and bone, down to her very soul.

Darcy leaned into his hold, her hands bracing herself against the side of his waist. The fabric of his suit was cool and smooth to the touch, and her fingers gripped it involuntarily. Hades's eyes dipped to her lips, and she noted that as his tongue licked his own, her insides twisted rather deliciously.

The night had not gone as she intended,

but perhaps she could end it better than she'd sought out.

She'd never kissed a god before.

Darcy leaned forward, closing the space between them as their lips brushed one another's.

A part of her expected him to pull back, be a gentleman of sorts, after all, the man—no, *god* reeked of sophistication, and Cate had made it more than clear to the both of them that any type of romantic relations was probably not a good idea.

She was not prepared for the way in which he kissed her back. He turned her around without haste, and she fell back against the door with a thud. He sucked at her bottom lip, taking it between his teeth before kissing her again, letting his tongue slide into her mouth without warning. A satisfied hum left her throat as she slid her hands up his chest and she could feel the definition of his muscles through his shirt. Her blood heated, and she felt warm all over.

Especially when his lips started to caress her jaw, her neck. Darcy's legs felt like Jell-O, and her head felt like she was in a dream.

Then suddenly, it all stopped.

Hades pulled his lips from her neck, and his body tensed.

She could feel the tension in the air as if someone had just played body snatchers with the god she was more than planning on inviting inside her tiny apartment.

"I'm sorry, Darcy, I... I think it best if I leave now." His smooth voice carried a hint of concern, of panic.

"Okay..." she choked out, not entirely sure what else to say. Her head was still spinning and she needed to make sense of all the feelings, all the sensations that were overwhelming her.

Hades pulled back as Darcy unlocked her door, opening it just slightly before turning once more to take a good look at him.

"It was nice meeting you," he said politely, as if he hadn't just had his lips all over her.

Darcy reached out to his front pocket and he looked surprised when she pulled out his post-it note pad. She opened the door and grabbed a pen from the cup on her end table next to the door.

Adrenaline coursed through her, her entire being still aflutter from their heated kiss only moments ago.

When she handed him back the post-it pad, she smiled.

"Until next time, H," she said with a wink before shutting the door, and only once she was absolutely certain she was alone and Hades was gone, did she let out an excited squeal and collapsed on her couch.

CHAPTER SEVEN

WHAT THE HELL has gotten into me?

Hades paced in the kitchen of his surface condominium, feeling a mix of emotions and thoughts he could not process.

He'd thought Darcy was attractive, and she seemed like a rather sweet girl, if he was being honest, and anyone who could handle Cate surely deserved their stripes.

Sure, he would flirt and take a woman home occasionally, but he always drew the line before things got too serious.

Before they wanted more.

He couldn't afford to let anyone past the gates to his heart. Not after what happened with Persephone. He would not give anyone that kind of power ever again.

Perhaps, I just need a good night's sleep.

Hades poured himself a glass of scotch, loosening his shirt before kicking off his shoes and collapsing on his couch.

It was just a kiss, nothing to write home about. You've kissed plenty of women, including Tenille. But even kissing Tenille did not feel like this, no.

For when Hades kissed the five-foot-six brunette, his entire being felt alive in a way he'd thought he'd never feel again.

It was like a shockwave, like a bolt of lightning, like somehow he'd been in the dark and someone finally turned on the light.

The feelings that overcame him were hard to fight and so he let them reign. He tasted Darcy with his tongue, his lips, let his hands settle against the curve where her ass met her spine, and he let himself disappear for a moment inside that kiss.

Forgot who he was.

Which was not like him.

He needed to be in control, yet Darcy had somehow managed to do what no one else was capable of doing, not even Tenille.

Which was why he most certainly should not see her again. Temptation, such as that, could lead to rather unsavory roads. Not to mention she was Cate's friend, and that in and of itself could prove to be problematic.

Hades pulled the post-it notepad out of his front pocket and looked at the scribbled notation Darcy had left.

Angelo's Pub, Brookside
Medieval Times, Greene City
Sunnyside Light Festival, Sunnyside

Hades twirled the notepad in his hand once before setting it on the coffee table, deciding he was ready to call it a night. Sleep truly did sound like a good idea and would likely right his brain, and if not, he was certain when he met up with Tenille everything would go back to normal.

***

ARIEL DAWN

The night air was quite humid for fall in Los Angeles, yet it was much cooler than the heat inside the Den.

The lines to get into Den Of Sin were quite long, and a part of Hades felt sorry for those who would undoubtedly wait in the line for eternity and still not be able to get in. It seemed Samael's club was booming with business these days. Of course, business for Samael was less about the fiscal numbers and more about the amount of souls he could sign over. Something he was very good at. The Den only streamlined the quota, took out the middleman so to speak, which was also good for business where Hades was involved. Higher quotas of souls meant more incentive for him.

He walked straight past the throngs of people waiting to get inside, and casually strolled up to the podium where a rather brutish looking demon stood like a cold statue against the lights of the Den with the precious, coveted list of those who would be allowed within the Den itself.

"Evening, Jarol," Hades said coolly as a group of tourists exclaimed expletives at his 'cutting' the line.

Hades did not even blink or turn his head, unphased by their cries.

"Good evening, Sir. Long time no see," Jarol said as he opened the velvet rope for Hades.

The tourists cried again, and Jarol all but shushed them with a ferocious growl that would let anyone know, despite his features, he was certainly not human.

ARIEL DAWN

"Thank you, Jarol," Hades said nonchalantly as he rounded the hallway and entered the Den. The room itself was bathed in red lighting this evening, and though there were patrons milling about with cosmopolitans, flutes of champagne, among glasses of well aged whiskey, demons walked about in all sorts of costumes, most of them leather clad. His gaze roved over the galleys, settling on the stage which boasted an active scene with a woman who was bound with bright aqua blue rope and blindfolded, sandwiched between two of Samael's most popular performers.

Hades let his gaze wander over the woman, over the bright blue markings that offset the bronze tone of her skin, appreciating the care and artistry that the demons took in their Shibari.

"I expected you sooner, Sir." A lush voice befell his ears, and he could not help but smirk.

"I believe I am just as punctual for our appointment as I usually am, Tenille."

"Forgive me for looking forward to something," she teased.

Hades turned around, regrettably, from the scene in front of him, and faced the woman he'd come to know as his Mistress for the last several centuries.

She looked just as leather clad as the rest of the demons, sporting a leather bustier with buckles up and down both sides, and Hades knew well enough how many laces it had, how long it would take to untie them all one by one.

She flipped her pale blonde hair over

her shoulder and the curve of her ruby red lips was a welcome sight.

"Do you wish to sit and watch this evening?" she asked sweetly, as if she could have been from Heaven herself, but Hades knew better. He smiled in return at the Succubus.

"No, I do not think so."

Tenille extended her arm out and Hades took it into the crook of his own willingly.

"Then, let us find somewhere more private to play catch up," she purred in his ear.

Hades let Tenille lead him through the droves of mortals and demons, passing quite a few that looked oddly familiar. Then again, after a lifetime working in the pits of Hell on all scales, demons tended to start to blend together for him.

His job ferrying and sorting was more of an office job than most of Hell's employees and he did not see much interaction in his office. Despite being below the surface, most would classify his day-to-day life as boring. Drab. Dull. But there was an order.

Order and familiarity, which meant he was safe, and content. Free of interference.

Tenille was just another aspect of the way in which Hades assumed control of his life.

He passed Samael's demoness, Isabella, on the way, and though he did not stop to say hello as one probably should for a Princess of Hell, he was still not entirely sure how to take the human who had given up her soul, her own chance at salvation to be with a creature such as Samael.

The man certainly had his flaws, but yet

there was something quite intriguing, fascinating that someone such as he managed to carve out a piece of happiness in an otherwise cursed existence.

But Hades did not get to finish his wandering thought as Tenille pulled him through a door to one of the private rooms, locking it rather quickly.

The sound of the lock penetrated all other thoughts, awakened Hades as if he'd been asleep for the last few months.

His stature changed the moment he heard the sound; his spine straightened, his hands clasped behind his back as he stood distancing his feet two fists apart. He looked straight on into the room, which was lit with red lighting all around. Candles were strewn about the room while LED rope lighting lined the ceiling, and

Tenille swiftly walked over to the sleek black lacquered dresser in the far corner. Velveteen sheets and blankets draped over the large chaise in the middle of the room, and though he had become more than familiar with this routine, he still felt the shiver of anticipation down his spine as he waited for Tenille to instruct him.

To command him.

She turned to him, her fingers skillfully sliding along the leather handle of her riding crop, her long, shimmering black nails dragging slowly along the crop all the way to the very end.

"Come to me and sit. On your knees," she said with a crisp voice that was more clear than any bell. Hades did as she asked without question, kneeling in front of the chaise as he'd done so many times before.

Tenille sat down on the chaise leisurely, keeping her legs pressed together as she looked down at him, her blonde hair looking as red as a candy apple in the light. Her eyes had shifted from their usual sparkle to full on black.

"Good boy," she purred as he awaited her next command.

"Did you miss me, sweetie?" she asked with a glimmer of amusement.

"Yes, Mistress," he answered automatically.

He had missed this.

How it felt to let someone else assume control.

Tenille unhurriedly let the edge of her crop trace lines down Hades's arms, and he could feel it ever so faintly through the silk of his suit jacket.

"Remove your jacket."

Hades did as he was told and once the jacket fell to the floor, placed his hands behind his back once more.

"I did not say you were done," she hissed as she let the crop hit him against the arm. Though he was still wearing a shirt, he could feel the sting as if he wore none at all.

The pain subsided almost too quickly for his liking.

His gaze shot up to meet hers and he licked his lips, waiting for her to continue.

"Stand up. Remove your shirt and shoes," she commanded.

Hades stood and did as he was asked once more, watching the smile on her face.

"Good boy." She praised him and the tension melted away. His shoulders loosened, and it was as if a weight, which had been settled in his chest, had disappeared. Tenille stood, setting her crop down alongside her as she came up against him.

"Tell me, my dear Hades, would you like to play a game?"

He could feel the chill of the air against his skin; the feel mixed with the strands of her hair that tickled him against his nipples eliciting goosebumps on his arms.

"Yes, Mistress," he answered obediently. Tenille brought her lips to his, kissing him softly.

Hades's lips moved against hers swiftly, and suddenly, flashes of soft, sweet lips pushed forth in his brain. The memory was most startling to him and before he could react, Tenille broke away.

"What are your words, sweetie?"

"Green, Yellow, Captain," he said with a blink, the world falling back to normal. Though he knew the words by heart, it was part of their routine, if only for Tenille's benefit.

Being a Succubus meant that sexual or romantic situations were a transactional thing for Tenille. Every act, every physical feat would sever a part of someone's soul, and if they were invested in their enjoyment, one could lose themself completely, and end up committing their soul to Hell for the most enjoyable sex of their life. That was the payment. It was easy to lure mortals to the Den, to entice them to sign over their souls. But Hades had no soul, and therefore, there was nothing for Tenille to siphon or feel.

She could only ascertain Hades's feelings from his safe words, and from his physical body language.

"Very good, Hades." The way in which she said his name was a dark, pleasurable sound.

"Undress yourself fully and then assume the position," she said plainly, Hades nodded in response. He did as he was instructed, taking his time with his belt and zipper, sliding down his pants. The cold air against his cock caused it to twitch only slightly. He folded his clothes neatly in a pile and set them on the chaise before he walked with his hands clasped behind his back over to the back of the room. Tenille pulled back the red velvet curtain, and the light danced off the shimmering obsidian of the St. Andrew's

Cross against the wall. The silver restraints glistened ruby red under the lighting of the LED rope lights.

Hades stretched his arms out first, and Tenille fastened him in, her long nails dragging across the taut skin of his wrist as she did so.

It did not take her long to finish with his ankles, and she took her time dragging her fingernails up his leg, across his thigh, and finishing just over his torso.

"You are my favorite, you know that?" she purred in his ear, her lips brushing the spot of his neck that usually made him squirm.

But this time when she did so, his brain assaulted him once more with images of another.

With the memory of his lips upon the

slender jaw and neck of a lively woman who smelled of strawberry margaritas.

The action once more startled him and he jostled against the restraints. Tenille smiled, and Hades tried to shove the memory away. He did not want to think about such things. This room was sacred, the world shut out and locked away. Nothing from the surface or the Underworld came with him in the confines of his private quarters with Tenille.

At least, he had thought that was the case.

Focus, Hades!

"I love it when you fight," she moaned, her voice carrying the undeniable hiss that was prevalent in all Succubi.

Hades swallowed nervously as Tenille's fingernails traced the inside of his thigh before cupping his balls with one hand. He drew in a deep breath as she angled herself closer to him, grasping his cock with her free hand, her forked tongue darting out and licking at his neck.

It wasn't the first time she'd done such things, but something about this time felt... different.

Her hand tightened around him as she slowly started to build a rhythm, and his body reacted instinctively to her touch, her grip, the friction.

Hades leaned his head back against the cross, his eyes fluttering shut as sensation overcame him. The feel of Tenille's tongue against his flesh, of her grip on him, the warmth of her body as it closed against him was all encompassing. The darkness filtered in behind his eyelids, and it was a welcome return.

The nothing, the void.

The place between pain and pleasure.

But then, tiny fractals of memory pulsed to the surface. Bright blue eyes looked up at him, and the memory of a strawberry flavored kiss pushed forth and the fractals of memory lit up into fractals of fantasy.

Hades found himself dreaming of moans against his neck, of pouty lips wrapped around his cock that belonged to a vibrant woman he'd met mere hours ago.

The thoughts came like a hurricane, one after one, only interrupted by the hiss of a Succubi, and Hades lurched away as fantasy dissipated into reality.

"Hades?" Her voice caught with concern. "Where are you right now?"

"Yellow," he said through closed eyes, his skin heating up with alarm.

Tenille let go of his cock, and the cool air felt good where her warm grip had been. Hades took a deep breath, trying to come back to his center. It was not long before he felt the tip of her riding crop gracefully trailing down his chest, to his abdomen, and then along his cock. Though he knew the strike was coming, it did not hurt any less.

A strangled, frustrated sound escaped his throat, and Tenille did not relent.

She struck him again, against the flesh of his cock, and the memories snapped with pain, dancing in his brain like sugar plums on Christmas Eve.

Images of Darcy looking up from beneath him, her mouth wrapped around his cock, sucking and fondling him while he thread his hands in her hair pushed against his mind.

"C..." He tried to find his words, but it was as if some other entity had taken control of his brain, his capability of forming language of any sort. Tenille continued her lashing along his hips, causing him to lurch forward, the St. Andrew's Cross following him from its bolts as he did so.

"Where are you, sweetie?" Tenille said, her voice tinged in alarm.

But Hades could not find his voice.

Something was wrong.

Everything was wrong.

He pulled on his restraints, feeling panicked, his eyes still shut as he tried to make sense of everything.

HADES

"Hades..." Tenille's voice was soft as she touched him where his restraints held him, and the touch felt different.

Painful.

Not in the way it always had, but more like... it burned.

Hades's entire body reacted like ice reacts to a hot griddle, and the word left his mouth strangled and pained as the room shook. "Captain!" he shouted amidst the noise of shifting earth, of falling debris. The restraints around his wrists burst open, metal and all.

"Hades!" Tenille shouted above the noise, and before he knew it, her arms were wrapped around him, shielding him from what he wasn't certain.

But one thing he was certain of, as he opened his eyes and stared at the room around him in disarray, was that the Earth was not the only thing that had shifted that night.

CHAPTER EIGHT

WHEN HADES WAS certain the earthquake was over, he pushed away from Tenille's bountiful chest.

"Hades, what happened?" she asked as she reached out for him, but he recoiled from her touch.

Everything in his body chilled at the thought of her touching him.

Which was insane.

I've never felt this way toward her in the centuries we've done this...

"I, I don't know..." he said, trying to catch his breath as he stood slowly, looking around the room. The St. Andrew's Cross was upturned completely, and had come off the wall, all restraints broken. There was a large gash in the floor where it fell, wood splintered upward around the cross.

The lacquered dresser drawers were open in disarray, tools and toys littering the floor from the upheaval of the quake.

But none of that was what caused his blood to chill.

His eyes settled on the broken restraints, and he could see the smoke still curling in the air.

Blue smoke.

The remnants of his power.

Tenille wrapped her arms around herself, her black eyes had been stowed once more, replaced by her sparkling aqua ones.

"I'm sorry, Tenille," he said as realization of what happened dawned on him. He unfolded his clothes and started to dress, turning his back to his Mistress.

I did this.

Fuck...

I lost control...

"Hades..." Tenille was beside him now, and he could feel her eyes on him, begging him to look at her.

But he could not.

He had the nagging feeling he'd never be able to look at Tenille the same way again, and that thought both unnerved him and saddened him beyond belief.

"Hades, look at me," she said as she set her hand on top of his.

He looked at her from under his lashes, his shoulders tense as he buttoned his shirt.

"Are you okay?" she asked as her eyes searched his and he could see they were red rimmed.

"I... I am not sure," he answered honestly. Tenille pursed her lips, and it looked as if she was about to say something, but the door flew open and both of them turned to see Agramon, Samael's right hand man standing in the doorway.

"Everything okay in here? You guys all right?" he asked nonchalantly, as if there hadn't just been an earthquake.

Tenille looked at Hades before glancing back at Agramon. "Yes, we are fine," she said confidently. Agramon stood for a moment, eyes narrowing at Hades and the fallen cross behind him.

"Mhmm," he said with a twist of his lips, but he let it go.

Hades finished buttoning his shirt before throwing his jacket on, straightening his shirt collar.

"Hades, it is all right, all that matters is that you are okay—" she started to speak but Hades shook his head.

"I have to go."

Tenille did not fight him as he brushed past her, the motion eliciting a light wind that blew her pale hair like an angel in the night.

HADES

He did not look back.

As Hades rushed through the club, he noted the patrons and demons all chattering, inspecting areas of the club for damage. It did not look as if the damage had pervaded past their private room, save for the stage where a chandelier had detached from the ceiling, which was now hanging by one lone wire.

Distracted by the sights and his thoughts, he did not see where he was going or who rather he walked into.

The brush of a body up against his tore him from his melancholy thoughts, and when he focused on the woman in front of him, his eyes widened in surprise and his heart felt as if it would explode.

"Watch where you're going—" the woman said briskly.

No, it can't be.

Surely, I've been concussed...

"Wait, do I know you?" she asked, her voice clear as a bell. At the same time, her name left his mouth.

"Persephone?"

She did not look any different than she had all those years ago. Save for the attire that was prevalent about the Den Of Sin, she looked positively ageless.

"That's not my name," she said as she raised an eyebrow at him while pointing to an obnoxious name tag that read Hi! My name is: in large bulky red print, followed by a beautiful penned 'Belle.'

"Of course it isn't." His throat was suddenly dry.

"It's Annabelle, actually, but work said that's too old-fashioned or something."

The way she looked at him stung harder than any riding crop or whip.

Because she looked at him as if she truly did not know who he was.

That had been the price he'd paid for her life. She could not live in the Underworld for any length of time. A week, a month. Years. No matter how long she'd stay, she would lose years off of her life, and he could not be the reason for such a thing. No, Persephone—Annabelle as she seemed to have adopted the name now—needed to be set free from the Underworld, and in doing so, he had to sever her ties to everything in association with it.

Including himself.

Knowing she'd forget him, and everything they'd shared—it was the hardest decision he'd ever made. But seeing her in front of him, now of all times—he knew he'd made the right call. But that did not make it hurt any less. The sudden reality, the shock of where they were returned.

"You work here?" he asked in confusion. He'd never known her to be interested in any of the sorts of things offered by the Den Of Sin, but then again he didn't know her. Not anymore...

"Yeah..." she said curiously, cocking her head to the side as if to judge his sudden sense of stupidity.

"I—" Hades started to speak, but as soon as he saw Samael heading in his direction, he knew he needed to leave. The last thing he needed was to explain what happened to the angel, or worse—he'd end up spilling his deepest darkest desires around the man, and that kind of thing would give Samael too much power over him.

And if there was one thing Hades hated, it was giving anyone else even an inkling of power over him.

The only person he'd entrusted with such things was Tenille, and that was purely transactional and confidential, what with her being a Succubus and all. She didn't answer to Samael as the rest of the demons did.

"I'm sorry, I—" Hades found his mind spinning, and it felt as if the world was truly caving in on him.

Tenille, the earthquake... running into the woman who broke him apart at the seams, and Samael getting closer by the moment.

Hades felt his chest tighten as he took a deep breath and ran his hand through his dark hair.

"We will have to do this another time, Annabelle," he said as he pursed his lips before moving amidst the shadows, right beyond sight of Samael and every other creature of the darkness.

CHAPTER NINE

DARCY STARED AT the clock on the mint green wall in the waiting room of New Haven Animal Rescue.

Ten minutes left.

Ten minutes until Cate would show up. The goddess was rather predictable.

Darcy grounded her jaw in anticipation, the low-grade headache she'd had all day still hanging around like ivy on an abandoned house.

Yet, the thought itself was not an unpleasant one. It was the only reminder she had left of what had transpired the night before, when she'd stumbled upon Cate and Hades in the alley of the DeLux Cafe. When she'd been oblivious, not knowing what would become of it all. Not knowing that her night would have ended with margaritas and kissing a literal god...

The memory was more clear than it should have been. After all, she'd dreamed about it, about *him* all through the early hours of the morning, in the comfort of her king-size bed, amidst all her pillows.

Dark, inviting eyes and how they looked at her like they could see her very soul... Even thinking about them sent a shiver down her spine, but it was not a shiver of fear, no.

Not in the slightest.

And that kiss...

Darcy closed her eyes at the thought of Hades's lips against hers. His kiss ignited a fire in her blood she'd never felt before. How he tasted her, slowly at first but then crashing against her lips, her tongue, her skin like a wave all at once...

She blinked, trying to dispel the thoughts from her brain if only because she knew better. She'd likely never see the man again, and it wasn't as if she could say anything to Cate. Her friend had made her thoughts on any sort of relationship predominately clear when they'd been introduced.

She glanced back up at the clock. Five

minutes.

Darcy had every intention of driving over to Cate's this morning, but she'd overslept and then some. No doubt thanks to her three am margaritas and taco binge with the sexiest man she'd ever seen in her life.

Not only had she missed her alarm, she'd slept clear until ten-thirty AM... an hour past the start of her shift at New Haven.

She'd called Cate, left several messages. If it were any other person, she'd have been worried, but Darcy had known the goddess, Hecate, since she was a child. There was not much Cate could not stand against.

No, Darcy was more concerned about the shifter.

What was his name?

She let the thought dissipate as the door swung open.

Cate didn't look any different than she usually did. In fact, she looked much more casual, as if she hadn't given more than a parting thought to her wardrobe of jeans, a solid black tee shirt, and her gray cable knit sweater. Her long silver streak fell forward over her shoulder with the rest of her raven locks, some catching on the thick texture of her sweater. Her dual-toned eyes caught Darcy's, forcing her to sit up straight. She could still hear Sandy, Patrick, and Cindy in the back tending to the long-term animals who had not been adopted yet.

The tinkling bells on the door broke the silence, but the look on Cate's face was louder than any jingle.

Her eyes looked tired.

Darcy's stomach twisted.

"Cate, I've been trying to get a hold of you all day..." Darcy said as she stood up at the desk while Cate made her way slowly over.

"I know," the goddess spoke plainly.

"What happened with—"

"It is done," Cate said as she sorted through a pile of mail on the desk, never looking at Darcy.

"Is he..." Darcy could barely finish her sentence.

"No. He is fine," Cate said nonchalantly, but Darcy noted the faint tremor in her fingers as she said the words.

"Oh. Well, did you at least get to second base?" Darcy said with a smile as she nudged Cate's shoulder, trying to lighten the strange air of tension that befell them.

Cate huffed and rolled her eyes, and in a flash, the tension seemed to fade.

"Is that all you think about, Darcy? Your libido?" Cate asked with a smirk.

"I think, in this case, I'd be thinking about yours. You know what they say, you don't use it, you lose it," she said with a shrug.

Cate let out a small laugh, but her smile did not quite reach her eyes.

"I will disclose no such things," Cate said as she opened a letter, her eyes scanning the words quickly before she signed her name on a dotted line.

"You know, I never had any worry that things wouldn't work out. I mean, if anyone knows how to fix problems, it's you."

Cate smiled at Darcy's words.

"But if things didn't work out, you know you can tell me. And it doesn't mean you can't try again," Darcy said just as Sandy and her cohorts came out into the lobby with their belongings, ready to punch out.

"Got any plans tonight, boss?" Sandy said with the utmost cheer.

Cate narrowed her eyes at the woman who wore a smile that was so unnatural it should have been plastic.

Everyone at New Haven knew Cate was not a social butterfly. She was their boss, for starters, but she was also colder than an igloo in the arctic on most days. Save for the usual business things, Cate did not spend much time with the employees or the volunteers at the shelter, aside from Darcy, and she rarely went out socially, if at all.

Hell, the speed dating was enough of a rare occurrence it might as well have been a fucking blue moon.

"Just the usual. I take it you have quite the dance card lined up this evening," Cate drawled sarcastically, but Sandy never seemed to take the hint. She squealed in delight, and Darcy pursed her lips.

"Oh, Patrick, Cindy, and I are just headed over to Judd's for happy hour, of course," the blonde said excitedly. Patrick, her sidekick for all intents and purposes, nodded in agreement. He never argued with Sandy about anything, a fact Darcy was not certain made him smart or just overshadowed by the exuberant woman.

"How utterly mundane," Cate mused dryly.

"Are you coming with, Darcy?" Cindy asked inquisitively.

Darcy looked at Cate, unsure of whether or not she should answer, or if she should continue her courageous interrogation of the goddess.

As if sensing Darcy's predicament, Cate nodded.

"I'll be doing inventory all night, so don't let me keep you by any means." Darcy sighed, noting Cate's eyes seemed to have cleared up a bit, and her smile almost reached her eyes this time.

"Yeah, sure. Save me a spot? I should probably run home and change first, then I'll meet you there?"

The others nodded in response and Darcy forced a smile on her face.

Perhaps a night out was just what she

needed to erase Hades completely from her mind. As Darcy gathered her things, Cate settled in behind the desk.

"You sure you're okay? You don't want to talk about what happened at all?"

"My dear, Darcy, I know this may be difficult for you to comprehend, but sometimes there are no deep dives or convoluted backstories to things. Sometimes, things are simple. I did what I set out to do. I woke him up, and he left. That's all."

The tone in which Cate spoke told Darcy that things were likely far from simple, but she knew better than to press. If Cate did not wish to disclose the details, she probably had a good reason.

"Okay. But if you change your mind and want to drown your sorrows in a martini or something..."

"You know I am much more of a wine gal myself, darling. But thank you. If I need you, I will beckon you to my side with a whistle." She smirked.

Darcy rolled her eyes.

***

Darcy applied the last of her coral pink lipstick and smacked her lips together. Though her headache had started to subside, she still felt somewhat off-kilter.

She could not stop thinking about the dark and mysterious man whose searing kiss would be burned into her psyche likely for the rest of the foreseeable future.

"I just had an off night, that's all," she said aloud to her reflection, as if trying to convince herself of the words she did not believe.

Darcy tousled her hair with one final tease before grabbing her glittery pink purse and keys to head out the door to Judd's just as her Uber driver pulled up.

She slid across the backseat, buckling herself in, casually making conversation with the driver if only to keep her mind from wandering to dark eyes and sinful lips that seemed to permeate her brain today.

When the car pulled up to the curb of Judd's, Darcy stood for a moment on the sidewalk and took in the sight of the crowded street.

Tourists and locals alike walked up and down the street in loud, chattering groups while other individuals in high-end business suits bristled past on cell phones, all too entranced with their jobs to notice the passersby who traversed out of the bars onto the expansive sidewalk.

Music could be heard in the air, mingling genres together as if all the bars had gotten together to create an ADHD infused remix of rap, soul, and energetic pop with the catcalls and high-pitched squeals of those partaking in Karaoke at one of the bars closest to Judd's.

It truly was a rather busy, lively environment, and Darcy felt at home in the chaos.

Yes, this is exactly what I need to clear my head.

She smiled as she made her way past the throngs of people through the narrow entryway, flashing her ID at the bouncer who sat on a stool outside Judd's.

"Evening, Miss Little," the bouncer said

nonchalantly.

"Evening, Bruno," she said as she leaned in and gave the man a hug.

Bruno did not return the gesture, but she noted the smile on his face nonetheless.

"Try not to get into too much trouble tonight, eh?" he said with a smirk as he opened the door for her. Darcy cast him a smile as she winked at him.

"Oh, but trouble is my middle name, didn't you know that?" She feigned her best attempt at a British accent and Bruno only rolled his eyes.

"Yeah, yeah..." His words dissipated as she made her way into the bar, her eyes scanning the thick crowd of people for her co-workers.

Sure enough, she found them all

loitering about by the billiards.

Sandy was already launching into what looked like a spiel about something Darcy would find most boring, Patrick looking all too engrossed in her tale, nonetheless, as he waited his turn.

"Please, tell me that the drink in your hand is the one you ordered for me before I got here," she teased the six-foot-one teddy bear of a man.

Patrick may have looked intimidating to most with his stocky frame and lumberjack attire, but he was by far one of the sweetest men she'd ever met. His only fault was his more than noticeable crush on Sandy, who was either blind or dumb about the whole matter. Darcy wasn't sure which it was, but she had her bets it was the latter.

"I'm afraid not," he said with a twist of

his lips.

Darcy rolled her eyes.

"What the hell did I come here for then?"

"To be social?" Patrick said, raising an eyebrow.

"Please. I'm way more social than the rest of you," Darcy said with disdain.

"No, you are just a magnet for interesting stories," Patrick teased. "Speaking of which, how did the Speed Dating thing go last night?"

Darcy felt her blood chill instantly. What could she say?

Though she knew Patrick was no stranger to the unusual, it was one thing knowing shifters existed and another knowing that Lucifer was real and gods existed well beyond everyone's favorite G-

O-D.

"Ummm, it was... eventful," She swallowed nervously, hating keeping secrets, especially from her co-workers. They could smell a lie a mile away. She smiled for good measure, and Patrick seemed to accept the answer. She breathed a sigh of relief.

"I'm grabbing a drink since someone neglected to be a good friend and hook me up," she gave another eye roll as she made her way through the room toward the bar.

She sidled up in between two men, one who paid absolutely no attention, and one who reeked of what must have been far too much Axe body spray. The scent made her eyes water.

"Excuse me," she said as she squeezed past them, leaning across the bar as she tried to capture the bartender's attention.

The one who smelled of overpowering body spray smacked her ass, forcing her to turn in surprise and anger.

"Excuse you, asshole. Keep your hands to yourself," she bit out as she shoved him.

"I don't know what you are talking about." He snickered as he took a sip of his beer.

"Maybe that shit worked at whatever lowbrow frat you belonged to in your glory days, buddy, but—"

"Is this man bothering you, darling?" The velveteen voice that carried in the air elicited a shiver down her spine.

No, that's impossible…

Darcy turned her gaze behind her and had to blink to make sure she was not seeing things.

Because in the middle of Judd's stood a man in a rather fine suit, silk to be exact.

His dark eyes caught her gaze, burning into her soul once more, and Darcy felt a rather warm feeling in her stomach as moisture pooled between her legs.

Fucking hell.

Darcy had never been one to fall for damsels in distress, nor had she ever wished a man would sweep in and rescue her from anything.

She was raised against every part of those silly notions.

This man, this handsy asshole, was like many she had encountered before, and the notion, the stereotype that just because she was a small woman she could not fight him off was bullshit.

She had taken many self-defense

classes and was in her third year of Kickboxing. She could knock a man twice her size around if she really wanted to. If she focused hard enough.

But every bone in her body bent a different way under the gaze of Hades, and suddenly Darcy desired more than she ever thought she would.

"Yes," she said, never taking her eyes off Hades.

She watched as he slowly sauntered over, setting his palm on the man's shoulder every so coolly.

"I think perhaps you should leave." His sophisticated voice elicited goosebumps along her skin, and she pursed her lips together; as if such a thing could stop them. She'd surely start rambling anytime soon and ruin the moment.

No, Darcy wanted to enjoy this moment. Wanted nothing more than for this pain in the ass man to leave, so she could focus on the delectable god in front of her. The one she never thought she'd see again.

The man moved to say something, getting off his barstool. Darcy watched his shoulders tense, and then she saw it.

The flash of deep, sapphire blue flickered in Hades's dark eyes, like a lightning bolt lights up the sky.

The man in front of her stilled, and his eyes flashed with the same blue flicker, and his expression turned to pain and sadness, guilt flooding his expression.

"I was just leaving," he said almost robotically.

"Good. Now, before you part, I believe you owe this woman an apology," Hades said with a deep growl that Darcy felt all throughout her body, from her head to her toes.

"Sorry, Ma'am." The man nodded almost too politely. Darcy could not help the smile on her face.

"Mhmm," she said with a smile.

Within moments of Hades removing his hand from his shoulder, the man seemed back to normal, but as he glanced from Hades to Darcy, his eyes looked full of fright.

He all but ran out of the crowded bar as if he'd seen a ghost.

"Fancy meeting you here," Darcy purred.

Hades slid into the spot the man had abandoned rather smoothly. He gestured for Darcy to sit in the open stool and she didn't question an open seat at the bar. Hades brushed a stray strand of ebony hair back into place as he looked at her, his expression stoic like a statue.

"Yes, quite a coincidence," he said as he looked toward the bartender, catching his eye.

The bartender was over faster than Darcy had expected. "What can I get you, Sir?" he asked.

Hades scowled.

"I believe this lovely lady here has been waiting far longer than I. Perhaps you should wait on her first." He smiled that white toothpaste commercial smile once more and Darcy's lips twisted, her stomach full of butterflies.

Which was a new feeling for her altogether. No one, not any of the men she'd had the displeasure of dating, had ever left her feeling literal butterflies in her stomach.

Darcy couldn't help her smile as she leaned across the bar. "I'll have a Sex On The Beach, thanks." She wasn't sure where the words came from, after all, she'd never had a Sex On The Beach in her life. Usually, her go to drink was cherry vodka and coke. She wasn't one for fancy cocktails with umbrellas, mostly because they were always expensive, but she always thought they looked appealing.

"And for you, Sir?" the bartender asked plainly.

"I'll have a glass of your finest Scotch. Whatever it may be, no matter the expense," Hades said darkly.

Darcy absentmindedly positioned

herself closer to him, while still maintaining her seat on the stool.

"So, what brings you to Judd's?"

"I've a lot of my mind. Figured drinking alone would probably not help matters," he answered smoothly.

"Ah, well seems you've come to the right place, then," Darcy answered just as the bartender slid her a brightly colored concoction with an orange slice and a maraschino cherry on a toothpick. She frowned as she realized there was no umbrella.

"What is wrong?" Hades asked, cocking his head to the side.

"Ummm, this is going to sound so weird, but I thought it was going to come with an umbrella..." she said with a small giggle as she pulled the drink by the base closer to her. Hades set his hand atop hers, the touch sending a shockwave through her entire being.

Instantly, images flashed in her brain of dark, inviting eyes looking up at her, from beneath her, images of him towering over her, his sweat slicked chest sliding against hardened nipples and soft breasts. Of hands grasping her hips, fingers rubbing, tugging at her clit while being filled to the brim with his...

The images alone were too much to fight, and Darcy grabbed her drink with her free hand, shoveling the straw into her mouth if only to stop the moan of pleasure that threatened to spill out of her mouth as an orgasm rippled through her.

What the hell?

Hades looked at her with a hunger in

his eyes that called to every fiber of her being, and Darcy knew there was no turning back.

Not now, not ever.

In the crowded bar of Judd's, Darcy looked into the eyes of death and knew she was a goner.

CHAPTER TEN

HADES HAD SPENT the morning pacing about his kitchen, wondering if it would be better to call off his surface trip early.

He still had two days left before he was set to return home to the Underworld, and though he usually liked to adhere to his routine; he found himself in quite a pickle.

News of the tremor was on the local

stations of course, and though Samael had not come knocking on his door yet, he knew it was only a matter of time.

Then there was Tenille.

He had known Tenille for centuries, and trusted the Succubus with his deepest desires, with his pain. Though he'd spent ages assembling himself and his life into something he took pride in once again, he was not blind. He knew Tenille cared for him well beyond their contractual obligation, though she did not voice such things for fear of breaking their bond.

But if he had any doubts about where Tenille's feelings for him lay, they were all but squashed like a damn bug when she'd shielded him with her body, putting herself in harm's way to protect him. *Him*—a god.

Because, despite the contract being

black and white, despite all the efforts Hades had made to make it known to Tenille that he was not interested in anything beyond the service she could provide him, somehow the Succubus still fell victim to falling for him.

Which was a problem all on its own, never mind mixing in the fact that thoughts of Darcy continued to dance in his brain, and Persephone—or Annabelle—had also thrown him for a loop. He'd never intended to see her ever again when he had let her go, but some cruel entity thought it more than amusing to throw love, lust, and chaos into his otherwise controlled environment.

I need a drink.

Though Hades's bar in his condominium was stocked with everything he needed as well as his favorite rarities, he ventured that drinking alone about the state of his love life and his loss of control, would likely not end well.

Especially, if Samael or Agramon came knocking, knowing all too well where to find him. He was a stickler for routine, and aside from the places he liked to visit when on the surface, everyone in Hell knew where he resided on the surface. So, he'd decided on a whim to walk the streets of LA, to take in the surroundings of life and find some dive bar no one would know about, somewhere overlooked. He could hide in the shadows, enjoy his drink and then be off to his home below the surface until the dead of winter.

This was why when he had settled on Judd's, a bar hidden amongst the long sidewalk filled with other bars and cafes, he had not expected to see Darcy, of all people, inside.

Was it purely coincidence?

Or was it fate?

Hades was not sure he could discern which it was.

Of all the bars in LA, what are the odds we are both here at the same time?

There she stood in a pair of tight, dark wash jeans and sharp, black stilettos, her juicy ass showcased as she perched herself over the bar. His gaze traveled up her spine, along the red tank top that had slits cut all along the back, showing an expanse of pale skin, and through such he could see faint markings of a tattoo he could not make out.

The man on her right caught sight of

her beauty as well, who Hades could feel the lustful energy emanating from. Before he could move a muscle, the man brought his hand down on Darcy's ass, and the sound of a smack echoed in the air.

Fury and rage tore through Hades in a most profound way that did not make a lick of sense to him, but nonetheless, he let it run its course.

The thoughts that pervaded him at the sight ranged from deadly to possessive, and in a flash, he found himself next to the man, angling himself between him and Darcy.

Her eyes caught his and Hades felt naked in her gaze, despite being entirely clothed and in a public setting.

It was all a blur to him as he set his hand on the man in question, forced him to see the pits of Hell, and all that waited for assholes like him should they continue their path of douchebaggery.

With the obstacle of a man out of his way, Hades found himself feeling a sense of relief, but also nerves.

Yet, he stilled them as best he could, if only to look confident and smooth in front of this woman who clearly had an unsettling effect on him.

Her blue eyes sparkled in the low light of the otherwise drudgey bar and Hades felt the sudden urge to reach out and touch her. To push her hair behind her ear, to pull her close. Close enough he could run his hands up her back, twist his fingers in her hair...

Hades blinked and shook his head, trying to capture the attention of the bartender instead. Thankfully, the man noticed and came over almost instantly.

Just be cool.

It's not like you've never bought a woman a drink before...

The fact that he was carrying on an inner dialogue with himself over something as trivial as buying a woman a drink at a bar said far too much about the power the alluring mortal already held over him, and his cock, if the tightening in his slacks was any indicator. Hades found the conversation with Darcy was not as difficult as he had imagined it would be. In fact, it had gone easily enough, he'd managed to keep a cool demeanor despite the fact his entire body felt alive with new vigor in her presence. The bartender dropped off their drinks and, in the midst of Hades reaching for his glass, his arm brushed against Darcy's. The motion put him much closer to her, and as she pulled her drink toward her, he noticed she was frowning.

"What's wrong?" he asked, suddenly worried perhaps he'd been wrong—perhaps, things were not going as well as he thought they were. Perhaps, she was bored.

"I know it sounds weird, but... I kind of thought there would be an umbrella," she said with a shrug as she set her hand on the base of the glass. The instinct that ran through Hades was foreign. He had the inkling both to soothe her but also to send the whole thing back, and to tell the poor bartender not to come back without a small umbrella included.

Which was insane.

Who does that?

Certainly not him.

Hades moved and set his hand atop hers, and the feel of it against his palm heated his blood once again.

His entire being felt flush from his head to his toes, and though the images that wracked his brain were ones he'd almost come to expect, Darcy's energy flared around her. Though he had been able to sense her baseline energy as he could with most mortals, the height of elevation was what surprised him. It was as if Darcy's emotion, her energy had gone from zero to sixty in a millisecond. Being able to sense heightened emotions was both a blessing and a curse to Hades. It was not hard to identify the type of emotion, either.

No, he could feel the energy around him, like a thickening fog of lust created out of his deepest dreams.

And if that was not enough, he could feel her pulse quickening beneath his touch, see the rush of blood to her cheeks as she blushed maddeningly, taking the straw from her drink into her mouth so fast he thought she may choke.

His cock twitched in appreciation as he watched her cheeks hollow, sucking down her Sex On The Beach much too quickly.

Lust pooled in his own abdomen, his eyes fixating on her delicious pout. He was about to speak when he was jostled by a group of people approaching them.

A loud group of people.

"Jesus Christ, Darcy, how long does it take—" A rather large, burly man stopped just in front of them, and he looked Hades up and down as if he were inspecting him for cracks or something.

"Patrick..." Darcy swallowed slowly, her gaze darting from the group to Hades, back to the group.

"Who's your friend?" a tall woman with flaxen hair cooed, her green eyes looking Hades over with interest.

"Uhm... this is Had—"

Darcy seemed to stop mid-sentence, and Hades could not help but smirk as he realized she was not sure what to say. Though, as he prepared to introduce himself, he was surprised when she finished the introduction.

"—en... Hayden..." She blinked, crossing her legs tightly as she sat up straighter, looking him in the eye with a smirk.

"Underwood. Hayden Underwood," she said the name with a smile, and it sounded passable. Natural.

Hayden Underwood.

How fitting.

Hades cast her a devilish smile of his own as he extended his hand to the mortals she apparently knew.

"Nice to meet you..." he said as Darcy took another sip of her drink before continuing introductions.

"H, this is Sandy, Patrick, and Cindy, my co-workers from New Haven." Hades watched as Darcy swiveled on her barstool, now holding her drink with both hands while she worked diligently to suck down all of her fruity concoction.

The raucous roar of the bar erupted around them as nearby sports fans started jumping and cheering, smooshing Hades smack against Darcy and her friends.

"I'm so sorry..." Darcy said as she gripped her drink, her blue eyes flashing at him.

"That's too bad. I'm not," he said with a smile and noted her shoulders relaxed.

CHAPTER ELEVEN

THE NIGHT HAD once again unexpectedly surprised her. She hadn't anticipated running into Hades again, and the serendipitous event had left her happy as a clam.

Though, that might have also been in part due to the drinks they'd shared, or the fact they were currently winning their game of pool against Patrick and Sandy.

Darcy let out a chuckle as she leaned over the pool table, taking her stance as she focused on the red ball she was aiming for. Hades came up behind her, and she could feel his stare upon the expanse of flesh above her jeans.

She was always aware of the way men looked at her, and he was no different.

But yet... he was.

Darcy arched her back further, elongating her spine and arms, if only to push her ass out further right against his crotch.

He shifted back at the motion, and she shook her head as she made her shot.

It was a close game, and they were winning by only two points. If Sandy managed to make her shot, they'd win.

Darcy hoped she'd sneeze or something and miss.

She grabbed her drink—she'd lost count after the third drink—and Hades leaned close against her side.

"Thank you," he whispered in her ear.

Darcy turned in surprise. "For what?" she asked, feeling the fire of his gaze once more.

"I can't remember the last time I had this much fun," he said with a genuine smile.

"Oh please," she said with exaggeration and rolled her eyes.

Suddenly, she felt fingertips setting on her cheek, pulling her face toward him.

His dark, inviting eyes searched hers once more, and the room was spinning. But Darcy was certain it wasn't from the alcohol.

"We win!" Sandy's squeal broke the air that hung between them.

"Aw man..." Darcy groaned.

The group said their goodbyes not long after, and Darcy noted the time was much later than she'd thought it was.

It was nearing eleven-thirty. She'd been at Judd's for nearly six hours.

I've been with Hades for nearly six hours...

All of a sudden, the nerves she'd thought she lost came crawling back as they watched her co-workers pile into their Uber and take off.

"Well, I guess that's my cue..." Darcy said as she punched in her location on her phone.

Hades set his hand on top of hers again,

but this time the onslaught of images did not push forth. Instead, his touch felt warm and she could not fight the instinct to look up at him. Against the night sky, under the streetlights of the city, he looked quite beautiful.

"I know a quicker way home," he said with a smile that caused her stomach to erupt into butterflies once more.

"1-800 Underworld Lyft?" she said with a giggle.

"I hear that there's one particular driver who is faster than all the others. I believe his name is... what was it... Hayden?"

Darcy's giggle erupted into a full on laugh as she slid her phone back in her purse and smiled at him.

"Touché, H. Sorry, it was all I could think of on the spot." She inched closer to him as Hades wrapped his arm around her waist, his fingers tightening in the fabric of her shirt, and once again Darcy felt the gravity of his hold, the air of his presence.

"Close your eyes," he said quietly.

Darcy started to feel as if the room was spinning, as if she could no longer speak under his gaze.

Normally, she'd respond with a sarcastic remark, some witty quip that would lead to a ramble. But she had no words for Hades.

She could only do as he asked, knowing what was coming next.

"Good girl," he whispered darkly in her ear as darkness consumed her vision, her head resting upon Hades's soft shirt, his arms holding on to her as if she were a life raft.

A cool breeze kissed her skin, and she felt as if they had indeed moved, if only from the sounds of the night around her that had somehow dissipated into the sound of buzzing that was always prevalent from the fluorescent lights in the hallway of her apartment complex.

"You can open your eyes now, darling," Hades purred, a slight tremble in his voice.

Perhaps, it was from the alcohol. After all, he'd had his share of drinks, too. Mostly scotch, but there was the one beer Patrick had ordered because he'd misheard the orders during another touchdown fiasco.

Could gods even get drunk?

Darcy found herself wondering this among many other things she was not entirely certain she wouldn't ask, given her current state.

She opened her eyes, and in Hades's own she saw something she least expected.

Hope.

Wishful thinking.

Desire.

"I had a great time tonight," he said as he brushed her hair behind her ear.

"Me too," she said as she swallowed slowly, her gaze dipping to his lips.

Darcy did not miss the way he looked at her lips, or how he had not yet removed his arms from around her.

Perhaps, it was the alcohol in her system, or perhaps, it was nothing but a reaction to the way he touched her, held her against him.

Perhaps, it was because she knew she

shouldn't, or perhaps, it was a mix of everything converging on her at once.

But she could not stop the words that fell out of her mouth.

"Hades..." she whispered his name as she slid her hands up his chest, resting them around his neck.

"Yes?" he breathed the words shakily.

"Isn't this the part where you're supposed to kiss me?" she said with more confidence than she truly felt at the moment.

"Darcy..." the sound of her name was like a prayer.

"I want you to kiss me," she said boldly, biting her lip, her mind spinning. Hades ran his hand through her hair, and she watched as he closed his eyes and licked his lips, as if he was fighting his own desires. "I think you want to, and I'm not sure why you're holding back, but you don't need to. We're both consenting adults, and—"

"It is not that simple, darling."

"Yes, it is. It's the easiest, simplest thing in the world," she said as she pulled him closer. His dark eyes gazed into hers, and in them, she saw a glimmer of electric blue. Like the hottest part of a fire, and she did not wait.

She took Hades's lips against her own, but this time it was different. His lips moved against hers with a hunger that was deep, as if he was starving for her.

She regrettably pulled away as she fumbled with her keys, opening the door and pulling him in.

Hades stumbled in after her, and she

couldn't help but giggle. The door shut, and not a second later, the lock clicked into place, and everything was a blur.

Hades kissed her once more, pushing her back against the door, boxing her in with his arms on both sides of her. His lips traveled over her skin, up her neck. When he pulled away to catch his breath, Darcy continued letting her hands trail over his body, settling on his waist, her fingers hooking themselves in his belt loops.

"I don't—" He breathed heavily, as if he were frightened, panicked even.

Darcy pulled him by the hand further into her apartment, stumbling over her own two feet, stacks of paper, and books, as she pulled him to her couch.

Hades collapsed on the sofa, and Darcy wasted no time as she kicked her stilettos off before straddling his lap, letting her lips scour his neck as she slid his suit jacket down his arms.

"What?" she asked between breaths and kisses.

"I don't normally do this sort of thing... I... need you to know that," he whispered as he met her mouth with his, his tongue caressing hers with need.

"Okay." She giggled.

Hades let out a deep sigh as his hands slid slowly down her spine, resting at her backside.

She took his earlobe between her teeth and nibbled lightly.

Hades let out a soft moan as his hands settled on her ass, his fingers tightening as he grabbed her.

The touch sent another jolt through her

system and she could feel a familiar moisture blossoming between her legs.

She worked at the button of his shirt, taking longer than she'd anticipated, no doubt due to the culmination of multiple Sex On The Beach drinks.

Hades slid his right hand around to her front, down her thigh. As his thumb brushed her mound through her jeans, Darcy could not help the moan that escaped her mouth, her hips grinding against him with need.

"Fuck... Darcy..." his voice darkened as he purred her name.

"Yes, please," she said as she opened his shirt, taking in the expanse of his solid, tanned chest. "God, yes, please..."

She was practically salivating at the sight, at the definition in his chest, his abs, and the delicious V that made her glance lower. And just as her gaze fixated on his groin, she noted the sizable tent in his pants, and the sight only emblazoned her more.

Hades pushed forward, grabbing her underneath her ass cheeks tightly as he picked her up. Darcy squealed with delight, another rambunctious giggle escaping her throat. He set her back down on the couch, much harder than she would have liked, but she did not care at the moment. For the speed in which he unzipped her dark wash jeans and had them down around her ankles was all she could truly focus on.

She kicked off the remains of her pants, flinging them to the far corner of the room, their landing unbeknownst to her.

Hades let his hands trail up her inner

thighs, let his fingers tug at the sides of her panties as he licked his lips. Darcy noted his eyes had dilated, the blue haze still ever present in them. His lips caressed the inside of her leg as he moved painstakingly slowly up to her inner thigh, his kisses leaving her skin flush in their aftermath. The anticipation built inside of her like a hurricane as she thrust her hips forward in response. Hades hooked his thumb underneath the side of her panties, sliding them down inch by inch for what seemed like an eternity.

"God, I don't know how much longer I can stand this..." Darcy whined in frustration just as she felt the overwhelming feeling in her loins pull to one particular spot.

Hades held her clit between his thumb

and forefinger, rubbing, tugging on the sensitive bead in a rhythmic fashion that caused Darcy's spine to straighten completely.

"Oh fuck..." she said as her head hit the back of the sofa.

"You like that?" he purred, his velveteen voice a power all on its own.

"Yes..." she moaned.

"Yes, Sir," he said definitively.

"Yes, Sir." She giggled, trying to keep a straight face.

Darcy had never been one for all the daddy, sir, master calling during sex, but she found herself all too willing to do as Hades asked.

I will call this man whatever the hell he wants as long as he keeps doing what he's doing...

She cleared her throat once more, trying again to say the words without giggling this time.

"I mean, yes, Sir," she said in the sexiest tone she could muster up at the moment.

It must have done the trick, because upon doing so she felt Hades pull her panties down to her ankles, and a warm tongue replacing skillful fingers. He lapped at her clit with the same rhythm his fingers had, and she could not deny it felt amazing.

But all of that paled in comparison until he slid not one, but two fingers in her soaked entrance and her insides tightened, her legs spasming at the overwhelming sensation.

"Fuck... I'm going to come..." she

moaned as her legs tightened against the side of his head, her breaths starting to come in quicker.

The orgasm hit her out of nowhere, and it was unlike anything she'd ever felt. She squeezed the sides of his head with her thighs, leaning forward as her hands found their way into his dark hair. She grabbed onto the soft locks with her fists, grinding against his mouth, his face, as she came undone.

When the euphoria of release had dissipated, Darcy felt as if she could pass out. Energy coursed throughout her entire being as if she'd been struck by lightning, every nerve, every synapse coming down from the high like a barometer dropping to below zero.

Her head lolled back against the sofa as

she tried to catch her breath. She was barely able to discern Hades had moved from between her legs and was now sitting beside her.

"Holy hell..." she whispered, still seeing spots behind her eyes.

"Close your eyes, Darcy." The way in which he spoke was like every dream, every wish, she'd ever made on a birthday candle had somehow come true.

"Yes, Sir..." she said tiredly as warm arms pulled her close into an embrace. Her head rolled back against a trim, solid chest and she could faintly feel fingers combing through her hair.

"Good girl," was the last thing Darcy heard as she drifted off to slumber.

CHAPTER TWELVE

HADES STIRRED, HIS eyes adjusting the low light in a room he did not recognize.

His chest felt heavy, and his arm had gone stiff from the position it had been in for lord knows how many hours.

He wiped his eyes with his free hand, noting he had a marginal headache.

At the realization, his whole body

tensed. His eyes widened as he took in his surroundings. He was on a bright canary yellow couch, neon pillows upturned all around from the initial collapse onto the furniture. His gaze fell to the woman in his arms, her head on his chest.

As his gaze traveled down from the top of her head, he could see she was still wearing her red shirt, but her pants had gone missing...

Then it all came back to him in a flash.

A lustful, hazy flash.

How she'd kissed him in the doorway.

The urges that she brought about in him.

Urges he hadn't felt for so long...

The memory of her hands roaming over his body, of the taste of her on his tongue.

The sound of her voice as she called his

name.

"What have I done?" he whispered into the silent room.

Panic and anxiety started to rise within him, and he could feel his power, his flames, dancing just beneath the surface.

He'd lost control.

Forgotten who he was, where he was.

He shifted his body, lightly moving Darcy, careful not to awaken her.

He carried her quietly to her bedroom, laying her down gingerly on the bed, and pulling up the throw blankets folded at the bottom around her.

Hades looked at the peacefully sleeping Darcy, every part of him feeling alive in a way he hadn't before.

The feeling was rather addicting, if he was being honest.

He shut the door to her bedroom, padding his way over the living room once more. He stood in the center, buttoning his shirt before picking up his jacket and slinging it over his shoulder.

"This can't happen again," he said to himself. "You need to get a hold of yourself, you are losing control."

He stood straighter as he took a deep breath and moved to open the door.

As he stood there in Darcy's doorway, his heart ached, and his head throbbed.

He closed the door once more, and within seconds, he was gone as if he'd never been there.

***

Hades exited the ferry to the Underworld just as he had every other time he'd gone to the surface.

But as he exited this time, he felt different. A hundred emotions coursed through him.

Shame.

Regret.

Joy.

Desire.

He'd been perfectly fine up until the moment he'd decided to attend Aphrodite and Eve's little establishment.

Lucifer had raved about The DeLux Cafe, and he felt as if it would only be right if he stopped by the place to check it out. It wasn't quite a recommendation, but he had mentioned it on his post-it note. Not to mention, he'd been delighted at the idea of flirting with singles, perhaps enjoying some drinks. Getting laid was not out of the question, but he didn't need the validation of such things when he had Tenille. His desires were managed.

Or so he thought.

He said his goodbyes to the ferryman and walked the rest of the way to his home.

Lucifer had done quite a lovely job of cleaning up the place in recent years, and the neighborhoods far more resembled that of those on the surface than most people would believe. With the vast territories of Hell, Hades lived in a more idyllic department. The lawns were perfectly manicured and landscaped. Though the flora down below was much more of the succulent and cacti variety, that had never bothered him.

Hades's A-frame home was far from ostentatious. While Lucifer and the other higher level demons and fallen tended to take up residence in glistening large homes that spoke to their hierarchy, Hades had given up such things.

There was no need for him to live in an obsidian palace alone and, without Persephone, no flowers would grow to make the place look like a home rather than a prison.

The decision to give up his luxuries hadn't been an easy one. But after she'd left, none of it felt right to him any longer.

Lucifer stepped in, and Hades knew he very well could have cast him out, knocked him down to the bottom of the totem pole, but he hadn't.

Instead, the devil himself let him stay, even provided him an office he could hide away in for the rest of eternity.

And that had been enough for Hades. He'd slowly built up a life again, day after day in his office, categorizing and sorting. Making lists. Cross-referencing last moments, getting lost in his work.

But he was never happy.

He was going through the motions, and as soon as work came to end, he was forced back into his life of solitude.

He stepped up onto the porch, waving his hand at the door. While some demons and creatures preferred keys and locks, Hades knew no one with any sort of sense would ever try and break into his house, if only because such a thing would land them a visit from Lucifer.

For all intents and purposes, their friendship had provided Hades more protection than he felt he was worth, but it was helpful, nonetheless.

When Hades walked into his home, it was just as he left it. It had only been a week, but somehow it felt as if he'd been gone for months.

With a flick of his hand, the lights came on, the fireplace lighting with just a snap of his fingers.

He sauntered over to his bedroom, steadily undressing as he went. Removing his watch first, then his jacket. He discarded his clothes into the black wicker hamper in the corner of his bedroom before stepping into the bathroom in the large open shower, turning on the faucets. The steam gathered quickly. After all, it *was* Hell.

No matter how spruced up Lucifer made the place, it was still hot, dry, and carried the ever present scent of fire and brimstone, even beneath all the pumped in scents.

Hades stood beneath the rainfall shower, closing his eyes as he tilted his head back.

Tonight was a mistake.

He took a deep breath as he ran his hands up his face, through his hair.

In the course of only forty-eight hours his best friend had finally left her cabin, he'd accompanied her and her unconscious date, met a woman who seemed to have an effect on him that he could not quite describe, caused a minor tremor at the Den, and ran into his ex—

What was Annabelle exactly?

Ex-girlfriend didn't seem like the right word, no. She was more than a girlfriend.

She was the love of his life.

Fine, ex-lover.

That would have to do for now.

When he'd tired of the steam and hot water, he found that he felt a little better.

His body ached, and exhaustion overcame him.

Hades towel dried his hair as he walked, discarding his towel in the hamper as he passed.

He didn't bother to dress as he slid beneath the grey bedding. The cool, crisp fabric was soothing to his flushed, warm skin, and his body instantly relaxed once his head hit his pillow.

Tomorrow, everything would go back to normal, Hades thought as he drifted off into slumber.

***

HADES

The room was dark, no sunlight penetrating the blackout curtains on his windows, the only sign to tell him it was morning was the aggravating buzzing of his alarm clock.

Hades groaned as he reached out, fumbling for the button to shut the incessant device up. Once he'd silenced the noise, he sat up, pulling himself to the edge of his bed, and placed his feet on the cold marble floor. The chill surged through him upon the touch, and he ran his hands through his dark hair, down his face as he sighed deeply.

He hated mornings.

His routine was second nature. He brushed his teeth, showered once more—if only out of habit for his morning routine—

dressed, and was out the door in record time.

The walk from his house to Underworld Claims—or as everyone in Hell called it, Reaper Row—was not a long walk. It took Hades no more than ten minutes to get from point A to point B.

When he'd arrived at his office, he could see Meg, his secretary, through the marbled glass window bustling about. He opened the door, eager to get on with his day.

"Morning, Sir." Meg flashed her green eyes at him with the same amount of excitement she had every day. The sight always unnerved him.

How can people in Hell be this happy about working on a Saturday?

"Morning, Meg." He nodded to her as he

stopped by her desk just as she stacked a pile of papers and neatly pushed them to the side.

"How was your trip?" she asked plainly, adjusting her black square glasses. Her copper hair was pulled into a messy bun on top of her head, little wisps framing her face. She blew her bangs out of her eyes with a huff as she sat in her new chair, swiveling back and forth like an excited child.

The motion reminded Hades of Darcy swiveling on her barstool at Judd's frowning at the lack of umbrella in her drink.

"Fine," he answered plainly.

Meg shrugged, snapping her gum. The sound was like nails on a chalkboard to Hades, but he put up with many of Meg's antics simply because she was good at her job. Which was keeping everything in order so he could do his job without interruptions.

"I tried not to overload you too much, but there seemed to be a mass influx over the weekend. Apparently, a bunch of souls got rerouted because there was some glitch in the angels' systems." Meg rolled her eyes.

"Ah, the angels. Always making more work for us." Hades smirked.

"Mhmm," Meg said as she took a sip of her coffee.

Hades entered his office and as soon as he shut the door, his eyes widened.

Sitting—or rather laying—in front of him, on his leather couch was a half naked Orion and a pale, golden-haired woman who was wearing his shirt, both sleeping soundly.

"Ahem!" Hades cleared his throat as a million thoughts coursed through his head.

How the hell did they get in here?

What are they doing here?

Do I have to change the fucking locks?

Orion's eyes fluttered open, and Hades crossed his arms impatiently.

"You better have a good explanation for this," he grumbled.

"Hades!" Orion sat up straight, his motion startling the woman on top of him, waking her as well. She looked at Orion then back at Hades, her own eyes wide with surprise. She opened her mouth but no words came out.

Hades watched as Orion ran his hand down her back, his eyes furrowed.

"It's okay, we can trust him. I promise," Orion said as he brought his hands in front of him, making a hundred symbols Hades knew all too well, but hadn't seen in quite some time.

The woman did not speak, but signed furiously with her hands.

Sign language.

Hades did not think twice about signing back. After all, he spoke several languages. Death was not akin to English alone.

"Are you in some kind of trouble, miss?" Hades signed to the woman, avoiding looking at Orion.

She started to sign back, but Orion stopped her with his hand. He looked at Hades with a mixture of worry and something else. Something Hades could not quite place.

HADES

"I need to ask you a favor, Hades," Orion said nervously.

Hades sighed as he sat in his chair, sinking into it with dread.

In all the years he'd known Orion—lived next to him, even—he'd never considered them friends. Though, Orion always acted as if they were. But even so, he'd never asked Hades for anything.

Before Hades could speak, Orion stepped forward. The blonde woman clung to him, her gaze fixated on Hades.

"I was wondering if you'd be able to get me into the Archives," Orion said boldly.

Hades's eyebrows shot up in surprise. Access to Hell's Archives was limited to a handful of inhabitants. The only individuals aside from Lucifer and himself who had access were Azazel, Samael,

Azreal, and Samyaza.

And for good reason.

The artifacts locked up in Hell's Archives marveled that of the Angel's Archives. Some of the world's most cursed objects and most sought after historical items lay in the bays of Hell's Archives.

Hades found himself wondering momentarily if they would have a Diviner, like Gunner had possessed. Perhaps, that was to blame for his most recent odd behavior. He'd most certainly have to look into it...

"What do you need from the Archives?" Hades asked as he crossed his arms. He glanced from Orion to the woman, whose eyes were all but staring through his soulless body.

"It's not for me... It's..." Orion swallowed

nervously as he looked at the woman grasping his side.

The way in which his eyes softened upon her both instilled a surge of jealousy and longing in Hades, for he recognized that look all too well.

Love.

Orion what have you gotten yourself into...

"It's for her. Trinity." He said her name like it was a prayer, and Hades felt a twinge in his chest.

Orion signed fluidly to her as he spoke aloud to Hades.

Hades sighed, raising a brow at Orion. "And why does Trinity need to see the Archives?"

"She's a tongue-tied prophet. I... was tasked with finding her, to bring her to

Heaven, but I... I'm not so sure now. I think..." Orion focused his blue eyes on Trinity as he continued to sign. "I think she witnessed a celestial event, and that's why she can't speak. If I'm right, and we can find the right tablet, it should break the curse. Give her her voice back." Orion finished his signing and reached his hand out to Trinity, brushing his thumb along her cheek, and she looked up at him with a look Hades knew well.

Hope.

Perhaps, he could kill two birds with one stone.

He swiveled away from the sight of them, focusing on his computer as he turned it on. The light of the computer cast a bright glow on his features as he tapped away at his keys, punching in commands.

He checked the logs for the Archives, noting there were no scheduled sign-ins currently.

"Give me one good reason why I should grant you this favor," he said as he swiveled back to face the two of them.

"Because you know what it's like to have to make the hard call," Orion said as he looked at him, his eyes full of pain and love.

His words hit Hades in the chest.

He understood all too well what Orion meant.

No one had the gall to speak to him about the day he let Persephone—Annabelle—go. He did not like to think about it either. Hell, he'd spent the last several centuries burying those memories, trying to find a semblance of normalcy again, and he had. The memories pushed forth, and Hades, for once, could not fight them.

Hades gripped onto the side of the ferry, his knuckles white. Every nerve in his body stood at attention, every muscle aching with longing to touch her, hold her, tell her it was all going to be alright. But he'd never have that moment again. He'd never run his fingers through her silvery-blonde hair, never kiss her soft, pliable lips, or smell the scent of roses and lilies without thinking of her ever again. He'd never feel her fingers in his hair, traipsing down his arms with a touch so feather soft it was like silk. He'd never hear her laugh again at his awful jokes, especially when no one else thought they were funny.

He tried to stuff down the pain, the

anguish, but it was no use. The tears came without warning, and the magic ripped through him. He refused to look behind him, refused to turn around and look at the woman he left in the mountains.

He prayed that when she woke up she wouldn't be scared or frightened. That some good Samaritan would help her find her way, and that she would walk the remainder of her years none the wiser to the life she'd had before.

With no memory of Hell, of how it was killing her.

With no memory of him.

It was a cruel joke of fate that he did not deserve. To meet someone such as Persephone, to fall in love. To know a love so deep it was rooted in his very being, his soul. But he would have no soul after he arrived where he was going, and he hoped that would dull the pain.

The thought of losing her, of losing the part of himself which held such love caused a maddening burst of blue flame. It surged through him and out his fingertips, his eyes, the pores of his skin. The energy rattled the Earth, causing cracks to form as far out as Sacramento.

He had built a sustainable, orderly life in which he was comfortable. But as Hades looked at Orion and the tongue-tied woman in his office, the tightening feeling in his chest warmed.

"And this..." Hades closed his eyes as he took a deep breath before continuing. "This is worth it for you?" he asked, signing as he spoke so Trinity would not be in the dark. She needed to understand there were repercussions as well.

Hades could very well get them into the Archives, but if Lucifer found he'd smuggled them in...

Hades wasn't certain how he would react, and that caused him some degree of nerves. Not to mention that Orion was risking a lot as a respected bounty hunter both with Heaven and Hell. If Heaven found out he was going against his orders or questioning their authority, he could have his title stripped. He'd be condemned to Hell for the rest of his immortal life.

"Yeah, Hades. She is definitely worth it." Orion did not break his gaze with Hades.

"Fine. Give me a couple hours to do what I need to do. You go home. I'll call when the clearance comes through. Might be a day or two. It is the weekend, after all," Hades said as he turned in his chair once more, away from Orion and Trinity.

CHAPTER THIRTEEN

DARCY WOKE IN her bed with no recollection of how she got there. She certainly did not remember waking in the middle of the night to pee and making her way into bed.

The light filtered in through the window, and she removed the blanket off of her, realizing she was pantsless. The night came crawling back to her almost instantly, and she had to hold her hand over her mouth to suppress her squeal of excitement.

Memories of Hades, of his kiss, his hands along her flesh...

Her insides twisted at just the sheer thought. How he'd dropped her onto the couch, his torturous lips as he brought her the edge and pushed her over.

She leapt off the bed, and threw on the pink fluffy robe from behind her closed door, venturing out into her apartment.

Her heart beat with anticipation.

What if he is still here?

Only, when Darcy opened her door to find her apartment was empty, the memory of his presence made known by the upturned couch pillows, a part of her heart sank.

She silently cursed herself for letting her mind, her fantasies, run away with her.

Of course, he was gone.

He must have carried me into the bedroom...

She sighed deeply as she headed over to the kitchen, opening her refrigerator and going about her daily routine of breakfast; reaching for the milk, before pulling out a box of Cinnamon Toast Crunch.

She sat at her kitchen island, pushing around the sweet cereal.

Last night was a mistake. It'll probably never happen again, so just be happy at least one man in your lifetime was capable of giving you probably the best orgasm you've ever fucking had...

Darcy chewed on her soggy cereal and

groaned. Her head was splitting.

***

When Darcy rolled into New Haven with a venti cup of coffee, Sandy raised her eyebrow at her appearance.

Though Darcy was dressed in her usual standard scrubs that were the norm in the rescue, she was donning large sunglasses, and her hair had been pulled into a messy bun. She was not wearing makeup either, for she just didn't feel up to the task with all the reminders of her previous night.

"Please, tell me you got that guy's number?" Sandy said giddily.

"Sandy... please, not now," Darcy groaned as she took her seat at the front desk. The Advil had not kicked in yet, and Sandy's voice angered her throbbing headache.

Patrick came up from behind with Cindy, holding a black lab puppy. Patrick scratched between the dog's ears and they took their place next to Sandy. The three of them had boxed her in.

"Come on, Darcy, that guy was a total dreamboat and he was super into you. Please, tell me you at least took him home..." Cindy pressed just as Cate came from the other end of the building, flipping the sign on the door to Open. She looked at the crowd around the desk and raised an eyebrow.

"Is there something I should be aware of?" Cate asked dryly, her dual-toned eyes glowing against her fair complexion, raven hair falling around her shoulders.

"Last night at happy hour, Darcy met a

guy," Sandy squealed. Cate's expression remained emotionless.

Darcy had always thought Cate's resting bitch face was goals. The woman rarely held a facial expression of joy or excitement.

"That's...nice?" Cate said questioningly.

"What was his name... Had... Hayden?" Cindy asked out loud.

"Uh-huh..." Darcy took her sunglasses off and looked through the appointment book.

"Rough hangover?" Patrick asked as he leaned closer with the puppy.

"You could say that," Darcy grumbled.

"Pet the puppy, it'll make you feel better." Patrick cast her a rueful smile.

"Thanks," Darcy responded as she let her fingers softly scratch the spot between the sweet pup's ears.

She had to admit, it did make her feel a little better.

For the moment, anyway.

"That's enough water cooler chatter, you guys, come on. Darcy doesn't look like she wants to talk about it," Cate said with authority.

"But—" Sandy protested, but when Cindy pulled her scrub sleeve, she relented.

Darcy gave the puppy one last pet before Patrick gave her a soft smile and left for the back. It was just her and Cate, now. Cate leaned her long pale arms on the counter, her gaze holding Darcy's attention.

"Are you okay?" she asked quietly.

"Yeah, I'm fine. Not like the first time I

took a guy home who left before breakfast or anything." Darcy sighed. She didn't really want to talk about what happened with Patrick, Sandy, or Cindy, even. But she certainly didn't want to talk about Hades with Cate.

She wasn't quite sure she ever wanted to tell Cate she'd let the god tongue-fuck her senseless. She'd take that tidbit to her damn grave.

"Okay, well..." Cate smirked. "If you decide you're not okay about it... we can get some ice cream later. Hang out and watch serial killer documentaries." Cate's eyes sparkled on the latter.

Darcy couldn't help but smile. "Actually, Cate, that sounds like a great idea," Darcy said before taking a long drink of her coffee just as the first appointment of the day opened the door and entered the facility.

***

Darcy loved Cate's cabin. It wasn't homey in the traditional sense a cabin normally was, nor was it luxurious and opulent. Instead, it was dark, yet strangely comforting. The whole place was done up in a theme of wood and stone, and the elements of both could be found just about everywhere. Dark plum, navy, and forest green were the brightest colors among the grey and black that perpetuated every room like English ivy. Cate also kept quite an array of artifacts and historical items on display like her cabin was some sort of home museum. Darcy had always thought the items were interesting, as some of them were older than LA themself.

It also didn't hurt that Cate's cabin was removed from society enough that it felt like a getaway every time she visited.

Cate sat down next to Darcy, two pints of ice cream in her hands, holding the spoons close to their respective choice sides.

"Pick your poison," the goddess said, nodding to Ben & Jerry's Cherry Garcia and Phish Food.

"I'll take the Cherry Garcia," Darcy said as Cate proffered her the pint and spoon.

She curled her legs underneath her, not even bothering to wait as she popped the lid off and dug in.

Cate raised an eyebrow at her, but she didn't say anything. Instead, she just turned on the television and started browsing for something to watch. The air was thick with unsaid admissions, and before Darcy could take another bite, Cate spoke.

"I slept with Gunner." Her voice was solid, unwavering, yet, Darcy could hear a hint of uncertainty in it. She set down her spoon and turned to her friend in surprise.

Well, that escalated quickly...

"Is that a good thing or a bad thing?" Darcy asked as she scooped another large spoonful of ice cream into her mouth. She knew it was best not to say anything of her own thoughts at the moment. She needed to gauge the gravity of the situation.

Did Cate regret it?

Was she upset?

"I... It was... what I had to do. I did as I said, I fixed him with my magic. But that magic..."

"Was sex magick?" Darcy raised her eyebrows and she couldn't help the smirk on her face at the idea of Cate actually getting laid. The woman never gave into anything. She'd watched her crush on volunteers or techs from time to time, but no matter how persistent Darcy was that she should pursue her feelings, Cate always stuffed them down, ignored them.

So, the realization that she had tapped into such a primal source in order to—do whatever it was she did—was more than shocking and intriguing to Darcy.

"Yes. I have not done that sort of thing in centuries, and it—"

"Yes?" Darcy egged her friend on as she hefted another spoonful of ice cream into her mouth, waiting with bated breath for Cate to continue the saga.

"I did not expect to feel... the way I did. But that does not mean anything more can happen. Gunner is a shifter," Cate said the words pointedly, and Darcy set her ice cream down in her lap for a moment, trying to understand.

What did that have to do with anything?

"Soooo... do, um... shifters really do it better?" Darcy leaned against her arm, thoroughly intrigued, a smile forming on her face.

Cate rolled her eyes, but let out a small laugh. The tension started to melt off of Cate as her shoulders relaxed.

"You are impossible, you know that?" Cate said as she tore her gaze from Darcy and ate a spoonful of her own ice cream.

"But you still love me," Darcy said teasingly.

Cate selected a show, and instantly, the dramatic music filled the room as she leaned back into her couch comfortably. They were a good half-hour in before Cate spoke again.

"I haven't felt connected to anyone like that in a long time," Cate said as she pushed the empty carton of ice cream to the center of the coffee table.

Darcy glanced over at her friend, though she didn't move. "And that's a problem, why?" she asked.

"Because I wish I could see him again, but I know it's better if I don't." Darcy's blood chilled at Cate's words.

"Why?" she squeaked out.

"Because he's a mortal, Darcy. A relationship between someone like myself..."

"Someone who is immortal?" Darcy said the words plainly, but as she spoke them she could feel the anxiety in her stomach pooling.

Cate looked at her, her expression one Darcy had never seen before. Her eyes furrowed, and in the green and blue irises, she could almost swear it looked as if they were starting to glass over, as if Cate wanted to cry. Which was unlike her.

Cate did not despair over anything.

Especially men.

"A relationship between someone like me and someone like him can never end well. We are not built for the same kind of life. He has a pack to run, a normal life to live, and I—"

Darcy placed her hand on Cate's and held it tightly.

Cate looked at where their hands lie and pursed her lips before looking at Darcy once more.

"I have seen firsthand the downfall of that kind of love. I watched it bloom, and then I watched it destroy Hades until he was nothing but pain and heartache. I do not wish to fall victim to that and I do not wish that for Gunner, either."

Cate's words sunk in.

She'd watched Hades.

Watched as love destroyed him?

A burgeoning desire lit within Darcy at her words.

Who had hurt him?

How had it destroyed him?

The man she'd met didn't seem destroyed or heartbroken in the least. He seemed rather happy, full of life. Certainly not downtrodden or standoffish or emotionally unavailable. Not to mention the way he made her feel...

"What, um... happened with Hades?" Darcy asked, trying not to feign nonchalance.

Cate's eyes fixed on her television.

"He fell in love with a mortal. I believe your legends call her Persephone."

"Bad breakup?" Darcy swallowed nervously.

"You could say that. He was so deeply in love with her, he would have done anything for her..." Cate's voice trailed off, tinged in sorrow. "She split her time on the surface, and below in Hell. But mortals are not built to withstand Heaven or Hell, even for short periods of time, so she had to leave." Cate sighed.

"So… it wasn't like a mutual thing…" Darcy pried.

"I tried to warn him. Mortals aren't built for the same things we are. Life is far more precious, they are more fragile…" Cate turned to Darcy, a haunting ghost of a smile on her face. "But nothing mattered because he loved her. And when push came to shove… Well, the very thing that gave him life and joy tore him apart. Love damaged him. Those of us who remember the aftermath… Well, he is a cautionary tale."

Darcy let the words sink in. The notion that he'd been so deeply in love with someone, that he'd lost someone he loved that much…

The thought made her jealous, but also… it made her heart ache.

No one had ever loved her like that, and she doubted they ever would. The kind of love that was literally legendary. So legendary, in fact, that people still knew the tale centuries later.

But certainly they could not be talking about the same person. The Hades she'd shared margaritas with, played pool with, laughed with—he could not be the same damaged, heartbroken man Cate was describing. It just did not seem real to her.

But Cate had no reason to lie, and she did not know of Darcy's sudden interest in the god of the Underworld. There was silence for a long moment before Darcy finally spoke.

"But you are not Hades, Cate. And Gunner is not a regular mortal. He is a shifter. That... has to count for something, right? Your experiences, Gunner's experiences... They are different, and if you decide to, you know, take a chance... maybe things will be different for you," Darcy said the words aloud to her friend, but she was not entirely certain she was not talking to herself.

"It is not that simple, Darcy, but I appreciate your support, nonetheless," Cate said as she turned the television up. Clearly, the discussion was over.

Despite the interesting case the host droned on about, Darcy could not find it in her to focus on the television. Instead, her mind wandered to thoughts of Hades, and the life he'd had with... her.

She found herself wondering about Persephone. What she looked like, what she was like as a person. What he was like with her as a...

Darcy immediately shut the idea down, not wanting to go down a road of torment. She refused to think of him with anyone else, if only to preserve the few moments they'd shared. Keep them intact as she locked them up in the confines of her mind and closed the door.

Tomorrow, she would start fresh.

No more fantasizing about deliciously sexy gods with soft lips and wicked tongues. She needed to forget Hades, and as she watched footage of the killer in the documentary, she vowed that as the police led the killer into his cell of solitary confinement, her foolish flirtations with Hades would be locked up, too.

CHAPTER FOURTEEN

WHEN HADES LOOKED at his desk clock again, it was well past seven-thirty. He'd spent all day researching the logs of Hell's Archives for the location of the celestial tablets, but also any connection or mention of artifacts, like the Diviner Gunner had. Though he'd made it through half the list Meg had forwarded him, he still felt as if he'd accomplished nothing.

He was no closer to answers than he had been before he walked through his office door to see Orion and Trinity tangled up on his couch.

I'll have to get Meg to arrange a cleaning.

Lord only knows what they'd gotten up to on that thing...

The thought of such things sent a shiver down Hades's back.

A knock sounded on his door, and he looked up, relieved to be rid of the intrusive, disgusting thoughts about the pain in the ass hunter.

"Who is it?" he called as he leaned back in his chair, closing down his tabs quickly.

"It's your favorite sibling," a sarcastic drawl answered from outside his door and he sighed deeply. This day was beginning to feel like utter hell, as if it were never-ending.

"Go away, I am working, Demi," he groaned.

She did not relent, and soon enough the door to his office pushed open. Meg raised an eyebrow at him from behind Demi, shrugging her shoulders in defeat as she picked up her purse. "See you tomorrow, Sir," she said with a smile that looked as if she was holding in a deep laugh. Hades scowled at her as Demi made her way into his office, plopping down on the couch immediately.

"Have a lovely evening, Meg darling," Demi said sweetly, waving at her.

"Mhhhmm," Meg murmured as she wandered out of the lobby, toward the elevators.

"To what do I owe the pleasure?" Hades huffed as he folded his hands in his lap.

"Well, for starters, you could have called and told me you'd come back home early." His sister crossed her legs as she leaned back in the couch cushions. Hades opened his mouth to speak, to tell her he would not touch said couch with a ten-foot ruler, but Demi cut him off.

"I don't care what your excuse is. Next time, just remember some of us like a little notice."

"Noted," Hades said through his teeth.

"I heard you made an appearance at the DeLux Cafe." She smiled.

"Word travels fast in Hell, it seems."

"Well, when you are a coveted piece of meat, yes, it does." She laughed.

Hades rolled his eyes. "I am not a

coveted piece of anything, Demi. You know that."

His sister sighed. "You are a catch. Do not degrade yourself, brother. It's about time you got back on the horse."

"I have had... relationships..." he defended. If there was anything Hades despised more than Orion, it was the incessant meddling his sisters insisted was concern for his well-being. Hera was always prattling at him about being alone, shoving tonics at him left and right to make sure he was 'taking care of himself' as if he were a child and not a centuries-old god capable of cooking his own dinner. Demi, on the other hand, had quite the fixation on his love life. She'd tried setting him up with friends, left him little notes about apps and meet-ups, insisting that no one really *wants* to be alone no matter how many times he told her he was not alone.

He had friends, and... people he cared about. He had Lucifer, and his sisters, Meg. Tenille...

Though, as he thought of the Succubus, his stomach turned and not in the way it once had when he thought of her name.

Demi rolled her eyes. "Tenille does not count, Hades. You pay her to—"

"Demi!" He ran his hands over his face, frustration coursing through him.

He wasn't embarrassed about his arrangement with Tenille, though he didn't feel as if the entire Underworld needed to know the details of his sex life.

Least of all, his sisters.

"All I'm saying is, I think it's wonderful that you've decided to start dating again."

"I haven't decided to do anything. I only went to the cafe to check it out because Lucifer would not shut up about it. I didn't even know there was a speed dating event going on until I got there." He sighed.

It wasn't a complete lie.

He didn't know the speed dating event was happening that night. He'd discovered that, upon entering the establishment, and though he could have walked away, he did not. Instead, he decided to stay; the idea of meeting people, talking and sharing drinks sounded more appealing than the speed dating part of the whole thing.

Yet, the night had gone in a totally different direction and his life had not been dull or boring since. He just was not certain if that was a good thing or a bad thing.

"And how did it go? Make any connections?" Her lips pulled up in a smile, as she anticipated his gossip.

"I—" Hades chewed on his bottom lip as he fought over what to tell his sister. "Cate was there." He shrugged.

Demi narrowed her eyes.

"Last I checked, Hell was still hot." Demi scowled.

"Believe me, I was shocked, myself. I did talk to someone, but I did not get her name. Very quick, this whole speed dating thing," he said cautiously.

"You did not get her name? What the hell is wrong with you?" Demi huffed in annoyance. "I swear it is like all the centuries of being single has rotted your fucking brain."

"Well, I did not get her last name." He

found himself strangely opening up to his sister, unsure why all of a sudden he felt as if he could trust her with such information. Perhaps, if he gave her enough, she'd drop the topic.

"Oh, well that is an easy fix." Demi waved her hand through the air as if such things were nothing.

"I beg your pardon?" Hades raised an eyebrow in response.

"Aphrodite and Eve keep tight records of everyone who comes in and registers for the speed dating events," Demi responded, looking at him as if the answer were quite obvious.

A list of names would be rather helpful...

Hades could feel the gears in his head turning already.

"Are you suggesting I simply ask for this

list?" he asked cautiously.

"I mean, if you really felt a connection to this woman, I'm sure you could persuade Aphrodite to let you see the list. In the name of love and all that jazz." Demi shrugged.

"And what makes you think she'll just give it to me? Aphrodite hates me."

Demi huffed in annoyance again. "She does not hate you. Seriously, Hades, don't be so fucking dramatic all the time."

"I'm not dramatic." He crossed his arms, letting out a deep sigh.

"Right, and Hell isn't hot, either." She rolled her eyes.

"Don't you have a bakery to run?" he growled.

"I hit a nerve, I see. Fine. But this conversation is not over," she said as she rose from her spot on the couch. She walked unhurriedly, stopping in front of him. "It is good to have you home," she said with a smile as she left Hades sitting in his chair, spinning over the thoughts in his head.

Why he'd told her about Darcy, he did not know. He was supposed to be forgetting about her, but something about what Demi had said... about the list.

He could very easily ask Cate for Darcy's last name.

Or phone number.

But the thought alone made him panic. He'd have to disclose why. Not that Cate wouldn't be able to figure such things out on her own, but he would also likely have to endure a lecture from the goddess, which he did not want.

HADES

She'd been there in the beginning, when he'd fallen for Persephone. In fact, she'd warned him of the dangers of falling for a mortal, of ignoring their differences.

While no one could have been certain what the prolonged exposure in Hell would do to Persephone—Annabelle—Cate had been right to worry. Mortals and Immortals were compatible, yes, but mortals could not withstand the very things that those like himself could.

Hades had lived in the Underworld for ages, unscathed. Unaffected. Although Persephone had lived in the Underworld for less than three years, it had poisoned her soul so much that it was literally killing her.

Hades knew the dangers of engaging with mortals. He knew the dangers like the back of his hand. But even knowing what he did, he could not fight the maddening desire inside of him, the nagging voice that begged to know Darcy's last name.

Certainly, I have more control than this.

He sighed as he turned off his computer, heading out the door once more. Yet, instead of going home, Hades decided to go for a walk. He walked and walked until he'd ended up along the River Styx, watching the flow of souls he'd sorted there through the decades.

And so Hades sat on the bank of the river, his head in his hands looking for the answer in the luminescent glow of the lost souls.

***

The night was darker than anything on the

surface in Hell. The darkness fell around his home like ebony curtains. The only light that existed within Hades's home was that of the candles spread about his bathroom. The power had gone out again in his department, a scenario that was becoming more and more frequent. Hades did not know why the other departments had not suffered as many outages as his, but nonetheless, he was prepared.

He ran his hands through his wet, dark hair, rinsing the shampoo out before grabbing his soap. The soft tinkling of his rainfall shower against the marble tiles was a soothing sound, and he closed his eyes, taking in his surroundings. The warmth of the water and steam against his skin, the scent of his soap and candles filling the air.

He ran his hands down his chiseled

chest, building up a soapy layer along his skin that ran down his body in rivulets toward the drain. He braced himself against the tile with one hand, leaning his body forward, letting the water rinse him, cleanse him.

It had been two days.

Two days since he'd come home.

Two days since he'd woken up in Darcy's apartment.

Three days since he'd let go of his inhibitions and given in to desires.

Four days since they'd shared tacos and margaritas, since they'd first kissed.

The thoughts of her pervaded his brain once more, and he let them come. For it was just him, in the safety of his home, in the darkness, and he was tired of combating them.

He'd never felt quite this fixated in recent years on anything.

Not since...

He did not let her name invade his thoughts.

Not now.

Hades let his free hand roam over his cock, tightening his grip. The memory of Darcy's kiss spread throughout, catching like wildfire. Soon, memories of a kiss turned to memories of sound.

The sound of her calling his name, calling him Sir.

The sound of her release.

Sound blended into sight, as the memory of Darcy straddling his lap, against his strained, aching cock pushed forth, followed by the memory of the moment he laid his eyes upon her glistening core. The sight of how wet she was made his cock twitch and his breaths started to come in heavier. Hades gripped himself tighter, thrusting against himself as he sought release.

The feeling of how she'd grabbed him by the hair, the taste of her on his tongue, like milk and honey.

The memories and thoughts soon carved a new path in his brain, and in the privacy of his home, alone in the dark, he let fantasy overcome him

His hands gripped her hips, his fingernails dragging against her supple skin.

Hades held her in place against him, and Darcy rolled her head back against his shoulder. She moaned loudly as he thrust himself inside her. "Hades..." her voice was strained, full of heat and desire.

Full of lust.

His right hand slid up her abdomen, fingers traipsing over hardened nipples as they made their way over her collarbone, resting around her neck. He could feel her pulse against his fingertips, quickening from his touch. His left hand slid down across her abdomen, fingers finding her clit. He tightened his grip against her throat, forcing her head to turn toward him, his lips seeking hers hungrily. Darcy let out a soft moan against his lips as his fingers tugged and pulled gently at her clit while he filled her.

"Mine..." he growled into her lust-filled kiss.

"Fuck..." he grunted as he stilled, feeling his release as it hit him out of nowhere. His entire body locked in place, and he could not help the sound of ecstasy as it escaped his throat. Sapphire flames danced on his skin as his climax peaked. He closed his eyes, the heat making its way out of him in every way possible—through his release, through his skin.

The feeling was all encompassing.

"Fucking hell..." he panted as he felt his muscles ease, all the tension leaving his body.

Hades shakily let go of himself, sliding down against the tile until he was sitting on the marble floor, watching the water circle the drain.

It was just a fantasy, you've had plenty of them...

Hades ran his hand through his dark hair, trying to catch his breath.

It was just a fantasy, but it was more than that. In the confines of his home, alone in the dark, he could admit that. He could admit the ache in his chest was not going away.

It was getting worse.

Though he'd tried to think of anything else, focus on work, the Archives...

He could not deny his thoughts wandered often to blue eyes and dark hair, to strawberry flavored kisses, and tiny umbrellas in drinks.

He'd managed his desires with Tenille's services. He'd only fucked her a handful of times in the centuries they'd been carrying on their arrangement.

The first time, he hadn't known what else to do. He'd never been involved with a Succubus or a mistress. He'd only ever truly made love with one person, who he loved so deeply.

Sex with Tenille didn't feel the same.

It felt empty.

As if it were only a means to a release and nothing else.

Yet, Tenille understood, and she'd been more than forgiving. She'd told him there were other ways, offered him something less... intimate.

And it worked.

It had worked for centuries.

Even the women he'd brought home over the years, he'd always stopped them before things got too far. Hades hadn't wanted to fuck anyone.

But in Darcy's apartment, he'd forgotten.

He'd forgotten who he was, forgotten his

pain.

Forgot that he had walls.

Instead, he'd given in to the desire to please her.

To taste her.

To feel worshiped again.

And when she'd called his name, he wanted more.

He wanted to possess her, feel her from the inside. Feel the warmth of her wrapped around his cock, feel the deep undulating current of something he hadn't felt in an eternity.

Hades buried his head in his hands as the water slowly trickled down the drain, just like his sanity.

It was impossible to have such feelings, such strong feelings for a woman who he'd just met.

A woman whose last name he didn't even know.

Wasn't it?

For the first time in his long life, Hades did not have an answer.

Only the startling revelation, that despite how long he'd gone without it, despite not having a soul...

Somehow, he could feel the seeds of love blooming in the depth of his darkness and he knew he was surely doomed.

CHAPTER FIFTEEN

HADES BRUSHED HIS hands over his one of a kind suit. The fabric was not one anyone could easily order, lest they were a master fabricator like Arachne. He rarely liked to wear such luxurious things, especially on the surface, but he knew he needed to look more than appealing if he wanted Aphrodite to even look at him when he walked through the door of the DeLux Cafe.

Which was why he opted for the priciest, most authentic suit he owned. He'd taken extra time grooming as well, making sure his facial hair was trimmed just so, sharpening the contrast to his jawline. Aphrodite enjoyed beautiful things and Hades knew, despite his upbringings and misgivings, he could be just as beautiful as the angels, if he wanted to be.

He walked through the doors of the DeLux Cafe at approximately eleven-twenty AM. The place was almost unrecognizable, save for the red curtains and booths. Everything was much lighter in color, with natural light pouring in from the street windows. People scuttled about with their coffees, pastries, and wraps while soft ambient music played in the open space. Hades made a beeline for the bar. The bartender was the same from the other night, he noticed.

"Excuse me, I am here to see the manager." He spoke in the clearest voice he could, even though there was no need to distinguish himself from anyone else.

"Eve?" The man raised an eyebrow.

"No, the other one," he said solidly.

The bartender pointed down a hallway that looked darker than the rest of the floor.

Hades took a deep breath as he thanked the bartender and crept down the ominous hallway until he saw the white door with the ornate doorknob. It stood out amidst the rest of the place, and he knew, without a doubt, it belonged to her. Aphrodite. He tapped the back of his knuckles on the glass.

"Come in," she said sweetly.

Hades slowly made his way through the door, closing it quietly.

"Hello, Aphrodite." He forced a smile on his face.

"Hades, to what do I owe the pleasure?" she asked, not even looking up from her computer.

Hades cleared his throat as he strode over to her desk, never taking his eyes off of her.

She sat in her chair, her long dark hair cascading down her back in waves. The computer cast an ethereal glow on her fair skin, making the bright blue hue of her eyes look as if they were glowing.

Hades ran his fingertips along the edge

of her desk as he stopped in front of her.

"I have a favor to ask of you," he said darkly.

Aphrodite turned her gaze to him, her eyes roving over his getup.

"Has Hell really frozen over? I thought I'd never see the day Hades, god of the Underworld, asked *moi* for a favor." Her voice was rich with sarcasm.

Hades did not sit, forcing the goddess of beauty and love to look up at him.

He watched the smirk form in the corner of her lips.

Like Samael, the woman had the ability to make people open up to her. Divulge their desires, their secrets. The objects of their love.

Hades's instinct was to fight such things, but knowing the reason he was here, in front of her... Well, perhaps it would be easier to submit to her love spell fog and just let the truth roll off his tongue...

No, you need to keep yourself in control.

Only ask for the list...

"I can assure you the temperature of Hell is just as balmy as it is up here in this wretched City of Angels."

Aphrodite reached out across the open space of her desk, running her fingers over the cuff of his suit sleeve and in her eyes, he could see the appreciation. He could also see the glimmer in her eyes as she tried to pick up on what it was he desired. But he was more than familiar with gods trying to get past his barriers, and so he pushed back against her with his own energy.

"You've visited Arachne, I see," she said as she let her small fingers softly traipse up the sleeve of his suit.

"No one makes a suit quite like she does." He forced another smile, and Aphrodite pulled her gaze from his clothing, meeting his eyes.

"This better be good."

Hades took a deep breath and fixed his gaze on Aphrodite. His voice, much to his own chagrin, did not waver.

"I need to see your speed dating registration list from this past Wednesday."

Aphrodite laughed a deep, full-bellied laugh. Her eyes started to water and she shook her head.

"Did Lucifer put you up to this?" she said through another deep laugh.

"What? No. Why would you think—"

"Why are you really here, Hades?" She cleared her throat as she focused on him once more.

"The list. I would like to see the list from Wednesday night," he repeated, his voice carrying a hint of his annoyance. He leaned against her desk.

"You're serious." Her expression turned cold.

"Dead serious," he said.

"That's confidential information, Hades." Aphrodite smiled wickedly. "Why should I give it to you?"

Hades like snickered. "Because I'm asking nicely."

"Not good enough," she said as she turned in her chair back to her computer.

I'm going to have to give her just enough...

"I met someone at your... event."

Aphrodite turned once more, her eyes sparkling with amusement.

"Go on."

"Though, there was an... emergency and she had to leave before I could ask her for her contact information..." He twisted his lips as he said the words. Hoping they would be enough.

It wasn't a complete lie.

"Mhmm. You could just look her up on the internet like most people." Aphrodite shrugged.

"If I knew her last name, I would," he bit out. He was starting to lose his patience.

Perhaps this was a mistake...

"So you want me to divulge confidential information belonging to clients of the DeLux Cafe just so you can get your dick wet?" She raised an eyebrow.

"For fuck's sake, Aphrodite…" He balled his fingers into a fist on her desk.

"I don't think so. But this… this was rather fun, so thanks for that." She smiled as she turned back to her computer, dismissing him, and he snapped.

"Give me the damn list!"

"No."

"This isn't about sex, Aphrodite…" he growled.

She looked at him with a bored expression.

"It's always about sex, Hades. You of all people should know that," she said with a sigh.

"I know that you are a pain in my ass, and if I had another option I would not be here."

"Your compliments could use some finesse, you know. I'd polish up on that, if I were you. Catch more flies with honey than vinegar." She grinned.

Hades huffed angrily and spun around.

"This was a waste of time," he growled as he exited her office.

"Was great catching up, Hades darling!" she yelled as he left the DeLux more frustrated than when he'd arrived.

****

Hades walked through the park feeling hotter than a burning flame.

It was a lovely day, the sun was shining and the birds were singing, but his flames broiled just beneath the surface of his skin, and it took much concentration to keep them from pushing through the surface.

His meeting with the goddess had not gone as he planned and that had unnerved him.

True, he had other options to reach Darcy, but did he want to come clean to Cate?

Not really.

Though, it would have been far easier if Cate were more supportive of love to begin with.

She'd never been Persephone's biggest fan. She'd warned him so many times against coupling with mortals, against pursuing a relationship. He hadn't listened then, and he knew, even though the conversation would be the same, he would not listen now, either.

He'd barrel on through as he had all those years ago, blind to the feeling in his chest, drawn to the feeling of being with her. Counting down the hours to minutes and minutes to seconds until they'd be together again.

Had he learned nothing?

Lost in his thoughts, he did not realize how far he'd walked, or for how long. He looked around him at the wide-open space, at the individuals playing Frisbee, at the couples setting up blankets on the grassy knoll in front of a large screen.

A movie screen.

Hades could not remember the last time he'd been to the movies. He rarely kept track of the blockbusters that came out. Despite the fact people piled into the theaters, they were always quiet and left him feeling lonely.

Hades slowed his stroll and approached

a secluded bench underneath the shaded trees. He watched the mortals about the park, going on about their lives. Runners jogged alongside each other, mothers and fathers chased their children, couples laughed while eating lunch. Everyone had someone.

Everyone but him.

Why was fate so cruel?

Why did it seem the stars would never align for him?

He'd known love once, only for it to be taken away, and now...

Now, it felt as if he'd always be circling the drain, forever and ever chasing something that always managed to slip through his fingers.

Love.

A happy ever after.

Hades leaned his head back, closing his eyes as he breathed in the fresh air, hoping to dispel some of his melancholy thoughts.

Darkness shrouded his vision, and his shoulders tensed as he felt hands cover his eyes. His blood chilled, flames threatening to rise as every part of his being felt the sting of panic, felt an imminent threat. He'd been careless, and should have paid better attention...

"Guess who," a dark, sexy voice sounded in his ear and Hades found his hand snaking its way up slender arms, fingers trailing over the back of small hands. A soft giggle escaped her lips, and he could feel the heat of her breath on his skin.

Her scent filled his airways, sweet like honey. His cock throbbed immediately as he recognized her voice.

"Darling Darcy," he purred as he gently tugged her hands down.

She leaned her head down next to him, and he turned to see the sparkle in her blue eyes.

"Hi." She smiled sweetly and his chest tightened at the sight.

"Hi," he said with a smile of his own.

"If I didn't know any better, I'd think you were stalking me," she said with a giggle as she walked around to the front of the bench and took a seat next to him.

Hades's gaze roved over her petite form, noting she was wearing skintight, cheetah patterned, pink yoga pants, which hugged her ass quite nicely. She was also wearing a matching sports bra, with a sheer black, rather flimsy tank top. He shifted his stance on the bench as he leaned forward on his knees, if only to hide his erection for the moment.

They were in public, after all.

He cleared his throat, forcing himself to meet her gaze. His gaze traveled up her torso, settling on the perfect curve of her breasts, before meeting her bright eyes.

"Would you believe me if I said I was not?" He smirked.

"No," she said with a smile as she leaned back against the bench, never tearing her eyes away from him.

I could just ask her for her last name, her number.

I should be able to ask her but...

"How long are you staying?" she questioned, all traces of laughter gone.

"I beg your pardon?" he asked,

confused.

"You told me you came up here, what? A few times a year?" She leaned her arms along the back of the bench, her fingertips just gently brushing the edge of his suit jacket.

"Four times a year, yes."

"So, I've seen you three times now in the past five days. You seemed in a hurry to leave the other morning, so how long are you staying? Or was that just some excuse you tell all the women you take home?" She did not look at him as she spoke the last words.

Oh no, Darcy, it isn't like that...

Regret coursed through him as he realized just how it all must have looked.

"I... No. I was not lying to you. I... did have to leave." He sighed, letting his fingers brush against hers softly behind them. She did not move away.

I did not want to leave but...

"I left two days ago," he said plainly.

"But now you're back?" She spoke, staring straight ahead at the joggers running past.

"I had some... business to attend to."

"Mhmmm." Darcy twisted her lips, and Hades noted it looked as if she wanted to say more, but she did not.

Then, her entire stance shifted as she all but jumped up off the bench.

"Oh my God! It's Gunner!" she exclaimed.

Hades followed her line of vision, noticing the man he'd seen days ago in the back of the New Haven van. The man that caused Cate a great deal of panic, who had that energy...

Hades stood at the sight. He hadn't given much thought to what transpired after he'd left the man in Cate's care. Relief washed over him that his fate had not been an unfavorable one.

Cate had done what she set out to do. But as Hades looked at the large shifter, he could see something had changed.

For the way he held his shoulders, the glimmer in his eyes... Hades knew the look all too well

"Gunner, is that you?" the question fell out of his mouth without warning as he approached him, Darcy jogging behind him.

Of course it is, but—

"I'm sorry, I—" Gunner looked between them as Darcy came to a stop next to

Hades.

"He doesn't know who we are, H. He was unconscious, remember?" Hades turned to see Darcy's lips turning up in a smile.

"Unconscious?" Gunner's eyebrows shot up and he looked more confused than when they approached him moments ago.

"Forgive my manners... Yeah, I guess you wouldn't remember us," Hades said as he slid his hand in his pocket.

He noticed Darcy's gaze as it roved over Gunner, and he could not help the pang of jealousy, the flash of anger that traversed through him. His flames burned just beneath the surface, and he balled his fist in his pocket.

Why did such a thing bother him?

It wasn't as if he and Darcy were...

Were they anything?

Anxiety swelled in his stomach as he realized he could not answer the question.

He enjoyed her company, found her attractive, intriguing even. Intriguing enough she had pervaded his thoughts for days, but yet...

He was not certain if she felt the same, and that left him more anxious than he wanted to be.

Darcy flashed him an alluring smile before she continued speaking. "We are friends of Cate's."

"You are friends of Cate's?" Gunner stood straighter, and Hades noted his eyes were clearer at the mention of her name. As if just hearing her name could soothe something inside of him no one else could see or feel.

Some internal turmoil or damage.

Darcy nodded, the motion forcing her dark hair forward over her fair shoulder.

"I'm Darcy, and this here is—" Darcy turned toward Hades, a smirk on her face. "H," she said plainly.

Hades could not help the smile forming on his own face. He was only slightly disappointed she hadn't gone with Hayden again. He found he did not dislike the name.

He noticed then, that Gunner was holding a beer, and as he took a swig of it said, "That short for something?"

Hades let out a chuckle, suddenly feeling more confident standing opposite the shifter. His fire still burned beneath the surface, but it wasn't an anxious, angry, or panicked feeling.

Instead, it was powerful.

Hades squared his shoulders back as he looked in the shifter's eyes. He could feel his fire, the energy pooling behind them and he knew how menacing it made him look.

"Hades." When he said his name out loud, birds scattered from the trees, and he did not miss the soft sound that escaped Darcy's throat. After all, she was standing rather close to him.

Had she gotten closer?

"Like the—"

"God of the Underworld? Yes. We've been over this," Hades said as he rolled his eyes, annoyed at the fact he had to repeat such facts over and over.

"Unconscious, H," Darcy reminded sweetly.

Hades watched as Gunner looked

between them, his gaze settling on Darcy once more.

"Do you—" Gunner swallowed nervously, Hades noted. He could feel the stirrings of anxiety around Gunner, and that intrigued him. "Do you know where I can find her?" he asked awkwardly.

Darcy looked at Hades with confusion.

Gunner had been unconscious when they'd left him with Cate, but she had done what she set out to do. That much was apparent as he was standing in front of them. He had to have left her cabin, found his way back into town...

"What do you mean, surely you know—"

"I know this is going to sound crazy, but—" Gunner reached in his pocket and as Hades started to speak, Gunner pulled out the Diviner from his jeans pocket.

Hades found himself speechless as the low hum of energy surrounding it reached out to him, lines of arcane energy swirling all around him and Darcy.

"But this rock—" Gunner held the shimmering moonstone up in front of them, and Hades could see the reflection in Darcy's eyes as they widened in surprise.

"That's the one from the other night!" Darcy exclaimed as she plucked the stone right out of Gunner's hand. Concern and fear ran through Hades at the sight. Mortals could not touch such things... celestial and blessed objects, cursed objects. Doing so could have catastrophic effects on those who didn't have otherworldly blood.

"Darcy, don't touch that!" Hades reached out instinctively, his fingers brushing the palm of Darcy's hand where the smooth stone lay, and upon its contact, felt flush with flame.

Fire spread throughout his veins, lighting him up like a torch in the dark. He could feel the beginnings of tremors begging to make their way up and out of him, begging to spread their cracks in the Earth beneath him. Energy swirled around him, dancing with the blue flames that surrounded him... and Darcy.

When she looked back at him, he could see in the reflection of the glowing Diviner in her eyes, the bright blue flames that danced between them.

But most of all, he could feel the energy, her heartbeat, the undeniable magic between them.

And he never wanted to let that feeling

go.

Because it made him feel alive.

As soon as it came, it went. The glow of the Diviner paled, and his flames ceased back into his body as if they were never there to begin with. Gunner cleared his throat, and Hades regrettably broke his gaze from Darcy.

"The Diviner predicts your mate," Gunner said solidly, and Hades could not help the surge of panic that ran through his entire body at Gunner's words.

Mate.

Hades had believed in such things once when he was young. When he was in the throes of passion and burgeoning love, but all that disappeared when he'd let Annabelle go.

Mates weren't forced apart.

Connections that deep could not be divided.

Yet, the words as they hit his ears resonated deep within his being.

"Cate is my mate. She—"

"Say no more," Hades said as he shook his head, finding his voice, his grounding once more.

"Really?" Gunner smiled, and Hades could see it was one of pure hope, pure happiness. Hades reached in his pocket for his post-it notepad. It was as if a part of his heart, a part that had been locked somehow, just... opened.

And flooding out of it was his own hope. That if, perhaps, Gunner was right about his connection to Cate, if they truly were mates...

Perhaps, he stood a chance at finding

happiness, too. If the Diviner was truly right about this... it could be right about him... and Darcy.

As Hades jotted down the things he knew Cate loved, would respond to, he hoped, prayed even though he was right.

"I can't believe you keep post-it notes on you..." Darcy teased him as she rolled her eyes.

"When I come topside, yes," he answered with a smile, knowing she knew this already. Yet, the way she said it was not judgmental, but lighthearted. Humorous even.

"So I can write down all the things I didn't do. Things I can do next time." His mind wandered to the scribbled notations she'd left the first time they'd kissed. The post-it was still on his coffee table in his surface condominium. He'd have to stop by to grab it before he left.

To look at it once more.

"Can't you use a phone like a normal person?" She poked him in the arm as she leaned close to him, looking at what he wrote. The motion brought her so close to him he could smell the faint scent of shampoo in her hair.

Coconut and vanilla.

The smell was rather sweet and pleasant.

It suits her.

Hades cast his dark eyes at her, and she caught his gaze. "You imply that I am a normal person, Darcy. Surely, you know better by now. I am far from normal." He smirked at her devilishly, feeling a newfound sense of confidence. As if the energy of the Diviner was still running through him, flames catching from dying embers.

Gunner's laugh broke the spell that hung between them, and Hades had to admit he had completely forgotten about the man standing in front of them. All he could see was Darcy.

"As I was saying before I was so rudely interrupted." Hades smiled back at Darcy before settling his attention to the shifter at hand. "I have known Cate for quite some time. If what you say is true, then you will need to do some worshiping. Cate believes no one can love her. Mortal or not."

Hades found himself saying the words quite freely, despite their weight. While most people tended to avoid Cate due to her rough exterior, Hades knew the real reason she regarded love the way she did.

Cate had never given in to love. She'd felt it, wanted it, even, but she had never acted on it. She felt as if she was damaged, as if she herself was not worthy of being loved. Part of that came from her life spent alongside humans who only sought her for things they needed, and discarded her once they'd had what they came for.

Years and years of such behaviors were responsible for hardening her heart, but if what Gunner claimed was true, if he really was her fated mate... then Hades would stop at nothing to see his friend finally happy, finally able to have the thing she'd secretly always longed for. The very thing she never thought she would have.

Darcy's voice cut through his hopeful fog.

"It's the immortality thing," she said.

"What?" Hades was not sure what she meant.

Darcy looked at him, swallowing nervously before she started to speak. Hades focused his gaze on her eyes. He noted the color of them reminded him of his own flames; a deep blue like the depths of the sea. They were quite stunning.

"The immortality thing. If you're mated to a god, and you're mortal..." Darcy broke his gaze, and his heart ached. Her eyes closed, and she breathed deep. The cheerful and flirtatious woman he'd become infatuated with seemed to disappear, replaced by something much more serious.

"Mortals die. We can't live forever." The weight of her words were heavy in the air between them.

Hades knew she was right. Cate had said as much years ago when he'd followed his heart without a care to the warnings of others.

She would outlive Gunner because it was how she was made.

Just as he would outlive Annabelle and Darcy.

But the memories would persist. They would live far beyond the mortal body.

But that wasn't enough. Not for gods like himself, or Cate, who would have to live with the reality that they could not hold or touch, or feel the energy of their love anymore.

At least, that was what he'd once thought, too. Now, he was not so sure. He'd always told Cate life was to be lived in the moment. Up until this very moment, he realized he hadn't lived at all. No, instead, Hades had locked himself behind closed doors, fearing he would become Icarus again and fly too close to the sun.

So close he'd be burned.

But what was a burn if not the physical scar that proved you'd touched the sun?

"Death is not always physical," Hades said as he looked over Darcy, his words true and unwavering. "You can be alive, but not alive."

Darcy looked up at him once more, holding his gaze. Her blue eyes searched for answers he was unsure he could give her.

But he wanted to so very badly.

"Think about it, H. You know her. She doesn't want to watch—"

Hades took a step closer to Darcy. Close enough he could reach out and touch her, kiss her. Tell her that none of that mattered.

But it did.

It mattered to her.

He could see that.

Images of their night at Judd's flashed in his mind. Her frown upon receiving the drink without the umbrella had ignited a desire within him to soothe, to fix. To give this woman, whose last name he did not know, everything she wanted, and as he looked into her deep, sapphire pools he realized the feeling was still there.

Only, it was stronger now.

He no longer *wanted* to give her the world.

He knew without a doubt in his bones,

in the very fabric of all that he was, he would.

Somehow, someway.

"There are deals that can be made, Darcy. Sometimes, life defies the odds," he said the words like they were a promise.

A promise to her, but also to himself, that he would find a way.

Perhaps, the answer lies in the Archives...

Hades turned and offered the post-it note to Gunner with a smile, and silently wished him all the luck. If he was pursuing the Keeper of the Wolves, he would need it.

"You'll only have one shot. Don't waste it," Hades warned. He knew better than anyone, Cate wouldn't expect a grand display and that alone would grab her attention. But the tightrope that led to her heart was far more difficult to walk. If the Diviner was right... perhaps, it would be the push Cate needed toward her own fairy tale.

CHAPTER SIXTEEN

SOMETHING CHANGED THE moment Darcy's hand connected with Hades's. The Diviner warmed in her palm as his fingers closed over top of hers, and suddenly it was as if every lay line, every atom, every road, and dirt path pointed to one place, one thing.

Him.

The connection she'd felt to him the night they first met—only days ago—was somehow so much stronger.

Like it was a force all of its own.

She looked up at the god, and in his eyes, she saw everything.

Everything that was, everything that could be.

But he was a god.

He was built to last for eternity, and if she was lucky, she'd live a long life well into her eighties and nineties. That kind of time was nothing for someone like Hades or Cate. They'd watched empires emerge and fall, watched society and civilization evolve, for god's sake.

Her heart caught in her throat. Despite knowing her life was but a glimmer compared to his, she knew with absolute certainty that nothing, no one, would ever be enough for her ever again. She only wanted him, and it didn't matter for how long.

She'd take whatever she could.

Whatever he was willing to give her.

Darcy shook her head as she watched Gunner walk away with a post-it note of instructions for wooing Cate. She hoped it would work. Knowing that Cate did, in fact, feel the same way, she hoped. She hoped that despite whatever odds lay ahead of them, they would live happily ever after for as long as life would let them.

Even if it was for a fraction of eternity.

Darcy's watch beeped loudly, pulling her from her fantastical thoughts.

"Shit, I need to go, my lunch is almost up," she said as she turned off the incessant beeping.

Hades only looked at her with a dark gaze that made her stomach tie in knots. He said nothing.

"Hey, um... you have a phone right?" she asked as the fog settled in her brain.

Hades looked back and forth, as if there was the possibility she was talking to someone else.

But there would never be anyone else.

Not ever again.

"Yes? Why?" He raised an eyebrow at her.

"Can I see it?" she replied boldly.

Hades pulled the sleek black phone out of his pants pocket and handed it to her with a shrug.

Darcy took a deep breath, her fingers tapping incessantly as she brought up his contacts. She furiously typed in her name and number, holding her breath as she did so. When she texted herself from his number, only then did she let out the breath she was holding. She handed him his phone back and winked.

"I have to go, but... it was good seeing you again," she said with a smile.

Hades glanced down at his phone before locking eyes with her once more.

"Until next time, darling Darcy." He smirked at her and the sight sent a shiver directly to her groin.

"Until next time, H."

Darcy picked up her pace, jogging away from the maddeningly sexy god and toward her car. When she got inside, her phone dinged.

"Are you free tonight?" The words could

have been from anyone, but coupled with the unknown number, and the feeling in her gut, she knew they could only be from him. Still, she could not fight the excitement blooming throughout her being.

"That depends. Are you going to hang around until morning this time?" She bit her lip and hit send.

"I could be persuaded."

Darcy grabbed her steering wheel tightly as her entire body flushed.

He's flirting with me!

"Well, I've been told I can be very persuasive," she said as she sent a kissing emoji at the end of her text.

"When do you get off work?" he asked.

Darcy started her car, music blaring through her speakers.

"Six o'clock." She tapped quickly.

"I will pick you up at eight o'clock outside Taco Tim's." His text was instant.

"K."

Her phone went silent, but as Darcy drove back to the rescue she couldn't help but feel like the happiest person in the world. She'd never been so bold as to put her number in anyone's phone like that. Usually, she just waited for a text or call from someone, not wanting to appear desperate or clingy if she contacted them a day or so later.

It was now or never. If Hades left, she might not see him again. It truthfully was serendipitous that, despite the size of LA, they'd run into each other. She'd been given three chances already, and she was not about to waste this one.

If she was going to pursue Hades,

pursue a literal god, she needed to up her confidence, up her game.

And so, Darcy did the only thing she could think of. She took the bull by the horns and put herself out there. He'd either accept and text her back, or she'd never hear from him again and she'd know it was all in her head.

He'd texted her back and asked her out on a date.

Of course, he hadn't said it was a date, but it was a date... right?

***

Darcy could barely focus the rest of the day at work. The day seemed to drag on endlessly.

Cate carried around a small kitten in the lobby, trying to soothe the animal after his most recent feeding. The poor thing was not quite ready for canned food yet. He was still building his strength up after he'd been brought to the rescue.

Darcy watched her friend as she ran her fingers over the kitten's soft fur, how her eyes looked at him. Despite her frigid exterior, Darcy knew better than anyone that Cate had so much love to give. And if anyone deserved a whirlwind fairy tale romance to sweep them off their feet, it was her.

Darcy approached Cate, who was now sitting at the desk, rocking the kitten back and forth. She pushed a paper cup of steaming tea toward Cate before taking a sip of her coffee from the break room.

"You should keep him," she suggested.

"Perhaps, I should get another pet. I'm

sure Belle and Spike could use the company," Cate responded, not looking up from the kitten in her grasp.

"I saw Gunner at the park today." She tested the waters. Cate looked up at her words, and in her eyes, Darcy could see the spark of interest.

"What?"

"You didn't tell me about the Diviner—" she whispered as she came around to the side, boxing Cate and her kitten in, but also making it so a gossip hound like Sandy wouldn't hear them.

"It doesn't matter, Darcy..." Cate sighed.

"I know I haven't known you as long as Hades..." Even saying his name out loud felt like drawing attention to her feelings, but for the moment she shoved the feelings down.

This wasn't about her. It was about Cate and Gunner. Her friend needed a push.

"Life is lived in moments, right? Isn't that what you always tell me?" she asked.

"I suppose," Cate grumbled.

Memories of the afternoon flooded Darcy's thoughts as the words fell out of her mouth without warning.

"Then fill those moments with love. All the little things, the tiny details..." She reached out to pet the kitten herself, noting its tiny mew as she did so.

"If all you have is today, Cate, make today your forever. Then wake up tomorrow and do the same," she said seriously.

"It's not that simple, Darcy," Cate protested.

"It is absolutely that simple, Cate. He is your *mate*," Darcy whispered.

Before Cate could answer her, the jingling bell alerted them that someone had come into the lobby, and they both turned to see a tall, muscular shifter with dark eyes and a wicked grin on his face holding... a bouquet of black roses? Darcy didn't even know black roses existed...

Darcy watched in awe as Gunner approached Cate. Watched as Cate's eyes softened, as her shoulders relaxed in his presence.

How he lit up with excitement, how his smile reached his eyes when he looked at her.

There was no denying the connection between them, even if you couldn't see the tendrils.

She could feel it.

CHAPTER SEVENTEEN

HADES PACED THROUGHOUT the bedroom of his surface dwelling. He wasn't entirely sure what overcame him the moment he'd realized Darcy had put her name and number in his phone.

Though, she'd only typed her first name. The verdict was still out on her last name, but with her number, he was certain he didn't need it, because now he had a way to contact her.

To find her.

Because she'd given him her phone number.

Bold move, darling Darcy.

He'd wanted to call after her, but he'd lost all control of his voice from the shock.

He wasted no time texting her, feeling a new surge of confidence at this revelation.

She'd put her number in his phone for a reason. It was more than apparent she did not wish to end their coincidental meetings, either. In fact, if the look in her eyes was any indication...

Hades stood in front of his closet, trying to decide on what to wear.

While he hadn't gone on a date in quite some time, he was certain the rules were still the same. One needed to make a good impression, and a good impression started with a good outfit.

Intrigued by the movie screen in the park, he'd decided perhaps it would be a good date idea.

Though he was not certain what movie would be playing, he was certain that whatever it was would not truly matter. All that mattered was that she said 'yes.' She agreed to see him again.

And that was the most important thing.

But as he stood in front of the suit he'd laid out along with the much more casual outfit of jeans and a black button down shirt, he felt his nerves starting to heighten.

And, as if he wasn't anxious enough, a voice, which should not have been anywhere near him, pulled him from his thoughts.

"I thought you went back to the Underworld."

Hades turned, his shoulders tensing, his blood chilling as he took in the sight of the tall, slim blonde in his doorway. Her golden hair fell in waves around her waist, and she wore a tight, black leather dress with heels that looked to be about six inches high. Her bright blue eyes caught his gaze, and he crossed his arms.

"You are not supposed to be here," he growled.

"I was worried about you," Tenille said as she pushed off his doorframe, sauntering closer to him.

"You do not need to worry about me, Tenille. I am a grown man, I—"

"We have known each other a long time, Hades. I am the last person you need to lie to." Tenille stopped in front of him and he could feel her energy emanating off of her, her tendrils of invisible desire reaching out for him.

But he would not fall into Tenille's gravity. Because he did not need her, want her.

She had given him peace for so long, but as she stood in front of him, he knew the door was closed on that part of his life. He did not want to stay locked up in a room trying to hide his pain. He wanted to leave that prison and be free.

Free to feel again.

"I have never lied to you," he said as he challenged her space, pushing her back.

Tenille reached out to him, running her

long, black fingernails along his cheek.

"You've always been my favorite," she said as her eyelashes fluttered, her gaze traveling to his lips.

"I know," he whispered.

"You haven't caused an earthquake since the first time we—"

The memory of the first time he'd had sex with Tenille threatened to come to the forefront of his mind, but he pushed it down. He hadn't known what else to do at the time. He'd missed Persephone, missed sharing a bed with someone. He'd never paid anyone for sex or favors before and wasn't entirely sure how the process worked.

It wasn't a terrible experience, enjoyable in the moment, even. Tenille gave him what he wanted, what he desired. And after years of all that pent-up sexual aggression, the flames beneath his skin were not capable of being contained. They'd radiated outward of every part of him when she brought him to the edge, tipping him over in sexual oblivion.

He'd grabbed her, held her with a force so strong he thought for sure he'd break her and it had felt so fucking good to let go. But afterward...

Afterward, he'd just felt worse. Empty, even. He still left and went to bed alone. Still woke up with an ache in his chest.

Hades wrapped his hands around Tenille's and pulled them away.

She swallowed nervously.

"You always let me touch you," she whispered in sorrow.

"I know," he whispered back. He didn't

want to do this with her.

Not now.

Not ever.

But he knew he needed to.

For both their sakes.

"Who is she?" Tenille's voice shook as she held onto his hand around hers, bringing her lips to his neck. She placed a satin soft kiss above his pulsing vein in his neck, and he felt...

Nothing.

What used to feel good, what he once anticipated, was no more.

"Does it matter?" he asked.

"Is it Annabelle?" her voice wavered and he could feel her energy pulsating with anxiety and fear, with pain.

Pain caused by him.

Because, despite their arrangement

being completely business and transactional, despite the walls and boundaries that lay between them, that he put up—Tenille had fallen for him. Perhaps, it was inevitable after spending centuries together so intimately.

Even for a Succubus.

The name made him freeze once it registered with his ears.

"What?"

Tenille ran her hand down his bare chest, fingers pulling at his nipples as she looked up at him with full black eyes.

Eyes that looked darker than the pits of Hell.

"I saw you run into her, I thought... I tried to schedule you on nights she didn't work, so you wouldn't see her, but—"

"What?" The words started to sink in.

"You knew Perse—Annabelle—worked at the Den? And you never told me?" Hades could feel the flames starting. All the things he told her, divulged to her, the things he let her do to him... because he trusted her... and she'd withheld this from him.

Knowing how he felt...

"I didn't think it wise to tell you given your history." Tenille tensed at his words.

"You lied to me." He pushed away from her.

"I protected you, because I—"

Hades took a deep breath as he tried to keep his flames in.

"Because why, Tenille?" He cast her a dangerous look.

The Succubus in front of him looked back with empty eyes.

"Do not make me say why, Hades..."

She sighed as she reached for him. He moved out of her way.

"I trusted you, Tenille, when I trusted no one else."

"Do not turn this on me. I did what was best for you," she snapped.

"What was best for me? Since when do you know what is best for me? You were my mistress, not my girlfriend, not my—"

Tenille's eyes filled with tears. "Because I love you!" she hollered.

The words echoed in the air, hanging between them.

"Tenille..." He ran his hands over his face, and he could not hold the flames in as they lit, dancing on his skin.

"Tell me you feel nothing," she said with a sniffle.

Hades looked at her, and he had to

admit he did feel something.

Sympathy.

He understood all too well the pain Tenille must be feeling. And so he reached out for her and pulled her close. A sob tore from her throat.

"Not anymore," he whispered as he ran his hands over her long blonde hair.

Her fingernails scraped against his skin, trying to hold on to whatever was left for her.

But there was nothing left.

He did not want her, need her, any longer.

"Was it something I did, something I said..." she asked through intermittent sobs.

"No. I just..." He took a deep breath before continuing. "I needed what you gave me. For a long time... you helped me. But now... now, I need something more than what you are capable of giving me, Tenille."

"How do you know I can't..." She looked up at him with tear stained cheeks, her mascara running down her face.

"Because I don't feel anything with you, Tenille. I never have..."

"But you feel it with her... with Annabelle?" She sniffled.

Hades let out a dark chuckle.

"No. Not with her either."

"Then who?" Tenille held her arms tight.

"Don't do this to yourself... It will not help."

Tenille's eyes fell over the outfits laid out on his bed.

"I'd go with the jeans. Your suits are nice but..." She sighed as she walked over to the bed, traipsing her fingers along the dark denim.

"Your ass looks good in these jeans." She let out a dark chuckle as she looked back at him.

"Tenille…"

"She's a lucky woman, Hades. Whoever she is." Tenille sighed and turned away. "I'm sorry. For everything."

"I know. Me too," he answered.

Hades watched as the beautiful Succubus left his dwelling, fading into the shadows forever.

CHAPTER EIGHTEEN

DARCY STRAIGHTENED HER hands over her dress, if only to wipe her clammy palms on the soft fabric, taking a deep breath. The walk to Taco Tim's felt as if it would drag on for eternity.

She found an open picnic table and sat down, trying to shake off her nerves. Her pink dress stood out against the rest of

Taco Tim's decor and she couldn't help but have second thoughts about the outfit she'd picked. In her apartment, she'd felt confident in her choice of the pink and black dress that she'd always loved but never got a chance to wear, but outside, even now the air was chilly and she was starting to regret her fashion choices. Her stomach flipped with butterflies as she waited with bated breath for Hades to show up.

Why am I so nervous?

It's not like I've never been on a date before.

Christ!

But even as she sat alone in the fading light, she knew the answer.

Because she hadn't felt this way with anyone she'd dated.

Ever.

Not that we're dating.

It's just… one… date.

And it hasn't even happened yet…

And as the realization struck her, she looked up, and there he was. Walking toward her like something out of her wildest dreams.

He looked almost unrecognizable, save for the dark hair and eyes. He'd traded his statement suits for a more casual look; dark wash jeans and a black button down shirt, which he'd rolled the sleeves up to his elbows.

Against the setting sun, his sun-kissed skin glowed with a golden hue. He looked downright sinful and Darcy had to blink to make sure she wasn't daydreaming.

"Well, you clean up nice," she said as

she slowly rose from her seat at the picnic table.

Hades smirked as he brought his thumb up to his lip, his gaze roaming over her as well.

Feeling his gaze on her caused her own body to heat in response. She slowly approached him until she was close enough to wrap her arms around his neck. "Why, thank you," he said in a low, dark voice that sent shivers down her spine.

"Are you ready to have some fun, H?" she asked as she looked up into his eyes, seeing in them endless possibilities.

"Yes, darling. In fact, I am," he whispered as he wrapped his arms around her waist, but this time his hold was not gentle. His fingers pulled against her back, forcing her closer against his body. His touch was... possessive. Before she could react to it, he said, "Close your eyes, darling."

She had never been an obedient woman, always needing to rebuke or question any authority or request, but when Hades commanded her to do so...

Darcy did as told without hesitation.

"Good girl," he purred in her ear as she felt a crisp wind, a gentle breeze around her. When she opened her eyes, they were in the park. The very same park they'd been at earlier when she'd come across him, across Gunner.

Darcy's gaze settled on the field, bathed in the oncoming dusk. Rows of couples and groups on beach towels, lawn chairs, blankets scattered about the lawn, ready for the evening showing in the park. Darcy realized only momentarily that Hades had not let her go, and she was still pressed against him. His hand rested at the small of her back, and she was acutely aware of the heat from his palm.

"You could have told me we were going to be outside. I would have dressed for the occasion."

"Oh, I didn't mean—"

"It's okay, don't worry about it. I'll manage." She smiled as she broke away for a moment, feeling flushed all of a sudden.

Hades slid his hands in his pockets as he nodded to a rather large tree a bit further from the rest of the moviegoers who were still coming in droves, laying their blankets, snacking away on popcorn, ice cream, and everything in between.

"Looks like a good spot to me," he said

as he headed in the direction.

Darcy followed him to see it had already been set up with a black blanket sprawled across the ground and a couple of folded blankets on top of it as well. She sat down immediately and noted the blanket was the softest thing she'd ever felt.

"What's the movie?" she asked as she tucked her legs underneath her. Hades sat next to her, extending one leg out while he brought the other up so he could lean his arm against it. The motion made him look young, and for a moment, it was as if they were just two mortals enjoying a fall date.

"I have to admit, I do not know," Hades said, his expression full of mock panic.

Darcy let out a laugh.

"You don't know? I mean, the tone of a movie changes everything. What if it's like... some civil war tearjerker? Or worse, what if it's like... one of those buddy cop movies that goes on forever?"

"Then, we will just have to find other ways to entertain ourselves, I suppose," Hades said darkly, and Darcy could not help the shock wave the words sent straight to her groin.

Well now...

"Are you hungry?" he asked, giving Darcy whiplash from the change in conversation.

"I'm sorry?" She blinked, shaking her head and trying to focus once more.

"Are you hungry?" he repeated sweetly.

Yeah, but not for food...

"Um... I could go for a snack..." she said with a smile.

Hades grinned back as he got up, and

the sight of him standing tall above her nearly took her breath away.

"Sit tight, darling. I shall return," he said smoothly as he turned around and walked away, off toward the food carts.

Darcy let her gaze roam over his backside, settling on his ass, which she thought looked rather good in the jeans.

***

A box of popcorn and Buncha Crunch later, Darcy could not contain her laughter. Hades playfully smacked her arm, rolling his eyes.

"Shhh!" he whispered, which only made her laugh harder.

"I'm sorry but it was funny!" she said as she tried to stop.

'I cannot hear what the possessed doll is

saying," he said with a chuckle of his own.

"I promise you, it's not important," she answered as she ran her hands along her arms. A shiver ran down her skin as the wind blew once more.

"You are cold." His voice had lost its laughter as he looked at her.

"Just a little. I'll be okay." She flashed the god a smile. The way in which he looked at her was puzzling. It was as if he was considering his words carefully. But instead, he did not speak. Instead, he reached out for her as he sat up straighter, gently tugging at the fabric of her dress at her hips.

Darcy let him pull her closer, and she shifted her body until she was between his legs. Hades shifted the blanket that was folded next to him, draping it over top of them, over her. His arms encircled her and so did his legs. Darcy leaned into him, bringing her back flush with his chest, her ass smack up against his groin. This close to him, she was practically cocooned. Warmth emanated from his body like a fire.

It was then that Darcy noticed the tiny blue flames flickering above the surface of his skin.

"Neat trick, H," she said with a giggle.

Hades let out a dark chuckle, his fingertips drawing lines down her arms, and despite being wrapped in a cozy fire, goosebumps prickled on her skin. His touch felt warm, soft, and pushed forth desires within her she could not fight. The thought of his hands, his fingers trailing over every inch of her body.

Memories of how they felt teasing the

insides of her thighs...

She could not help when her eyes closed, a soft moan of contentment escaping her lips.

"Is that better, darling?" he asked, his breath hot on her neck.

Darcy felt as if she was in some kind of dream. Wrapped in the arms of a god whose voice could turn her insides to mush, she wasn't entirely sure she wasn't dreaming.

"Mhmmm," she said as she breathed in the crisp fall air, breathing in the scent of fire and ash.

Hades.

She opened her eyes to watch the movie, knowing that the ending was near. She'd seen Chucky a million times as a teenager and practically knew the movie by heart, but Hades had not seen it, and his reactions were the most entertaining thing she'd seen in ages.

But when Darcy opened her eyes, she felt on the edge of a precipice. Her heart caught in her throat, and she was certain she was met with a gaze that was more compelling than any movie. The look in his dark, sexy eyes told her he was facing a similar predicament.

Her gaze flicked downward to his luscious lips and she watched as his Adam's apple bobbed as he swallowed nervously, while he stared at her with a dark look she couldn't even truly describe with words.

Was he nervous?

Hades tightened his hold on her, his right hand softly traveling up her arm to her neck, resting on her jaw; his long fingers pushing her by the cheek toward him so gently she was afraid she may have imagined it.

His gaze dipped to her lips, and she did not miss the hunger there, or the way her insides twisted deliciously as he licked his lips.

Darcy had never considered herself brave, or bold, but with Hades... she felt different. More confident. So she did not think twice about giving into temptation.

Temptation has a name and it is Hades...

Her fingers trailed over the warm skin of his arm, through the flames, which she realized did not hurt as she expected them to. Darcy felt herself slipping away into the waves of Hades and all that he was, and for the moment... he was hers.

"Much better," she whispered as she closed the distance between them with a searing kiss.

CHAPTER NINETEEN

HADES'S LEFT HAND tightened its grip around Darcy's waist as his right caressed her soft, chilled cheek. Her lips moved against his slowly, her tongue darting into his mouth eagerly. He deepened their kiss, letting his own tongue stroke hers in response before taking her lower lip in between his teeth, biting and sucking at the flesh in between softer kisses.

Darcy shifted in his hold, turning herself in his embrace. She leaned against him, snaking her arms around his neck as the weight of her torso pressed against his groin. His hands slid down her back, his left hand resting at the small of her back, hovering for a moment in its place.

Hades was acutely aware of the fire burning on his skin, of the steam circulating in the blanket around them.

Of the growing tightness in his jeans, the ache in his cock that could only be sated by one thing. And, as if Darcy could read his mind, she leaned further into him, her hands traveling down the fabric of his shirt, down his abdomen, stopping at his hardness. Her small fingers rubbed him through his pants and he could not help the moan that escaped his throat as her lips danced along his jaw, up his neck.

"Darcy..." he groaned.

"Yes, Sir?" She giggled.

"I think we need to slow down." He breathed deeply as he said the words, but the sound of her voice, the way in which she called him Sir... Hades could not deny the effect it had on his entire being.

"Why? Am I too much for you?" she teased as she took his earlobe into her mouth, nibbling and sucking at it, making his cock twitch. Instinctively, he thrust against her hand without thinking. The motion made her giggle once more.

"We..." Hades felt as if a fog of lust had fallen over his brain, and speaking was becoming rather difficult as all his attention was pulled to Darcy, who was now straddling his legs. Hades wrapped his arms around her waist once more, holding the blanket around them as she brushed herself against him.

"We... are in public, for one..." he breathed out as she kissed him again.

"Didn't peg you for the shy type," she breathed as her hands tangled into his hair.

"I am not, I just..."

"What?" Darcy pulled away for a moment, her eyes searching his and he could see the hint of worry in them.

"I think... before we continue... um... I need..." Panic had started to set in, and he needed to say this before it ate at him. Before things could be ruined.

"My safe words are green, yellow, and—"

Hades could not find it within him to

say the word.

Captain.

It had been his safe word for centuries, the one in which he'd used a handful of times with Tenille. But Hades did not want to think of his former mistress. He did not want her to poison this moment. So he said the first thing that came to mind. "Taco."

Darcy looked at him with a soft smile.

"Whatever happened to just 'stop?'" she asked.

"Stop is also good, but there are levels. Levels I need you to understand." He leaned his forehead against hers, and he could feel the steam heating in the blanket around them, the faint blue light of his flames steadily dancing on his skin.

"Okay," Darcy whispered as her fingers tugged at his hair. A chill wind blew, and the crisp air against his skin felt strangely comforting.

"What are yours?" he asked Darcy, all the while feeling as if her answer could utterly destroy him.

"Ummm... I don't have any," she said seriously. "But, I guess I could go with... green, yellow, and..." She let out a giggle as her eyes widened. "Mushu."

Hades pulled away, raising an eyebrow. "Mushu? Like the dish?"

"What? No. Like the dragon. From the Disney movie? You know, like 'dishonor on you, dishonor on your cow...'" Darcy said animatedly.

"Your safe word is based on a cartoon dragon?"

"Well, nothing breaks up the mood like a cartoon dragon voiced by Eddie Murphy,"

Darcy said with a soft smile.

Hades could not help but laugh.

"Where are you now?" He pulled against her waist, his hand sliding slowly down from its position on her back to over the curve of her ass. Darcy giggled.

"Green. Very, very fucking green. You?" Her lips found his once more and Hades did not hesitate when he kissed her with all the fire he could muster in the moment... which was not difficult.

"Green light," he whispered, though he could not deny he was nervous.

There was still quite a crowd, though they were mostly focused on the screen in front of them and not at all focused anywhere in their direction. But as Darcy thrust against the aching hardness in his jeans, his hands slid up underneath her skirt, feeling her soft flesh. He found himself pushing such thoughts to the side.

"Have..." He breathed deep as he broke away from her lips. "Have you ever been spanked before?" he asked, trying to catch his breath as his fingers stroked her soft skin, and he noted the expanse of exposed skin meant she was likely wearing a thong. The realization made his cock twitch, and his palm itch.

"You mean like sexually? Yeah, who hasn't?" she retorted while her fingers started to work at the buttons of his jeans.

On screen, someone let out a scream that filled the air.

Hades let out a dark laugh. "Did you like it?"

"I mean, I guess I did," she said between breaths. "Why? Do you want to smack my ass, H?" she teased him haughtily.

"Yes," he breathed the word against her, the lust inside him percolating like a coffeepot in the middle of brewing.

"Then, do it. Smack my ass, Sir."

It was as if the words unlocked some part of him he hadn't remembered imprisoning.

Hades did not think twice when he brought his hand against her, the crisp sound of a slap as his hand made contact with her flesh ignited his fire, and his entire body reacted with two emotions. Lust, and… relief.

And when Darcy cried out, biting at his lip, her tongue stroking his in response as she unzipped his pants, he could not help the wicked grin that spread across his face.

"You do not tell me what to do, darling,"

he said darkly.

"Oh really?" She tugged at his pants, but he did not move, forcing her to look up at him. The pout on her face was most endearing, and he could not help but feel powerless to it.

"I tell you what to do," he said as he licked his lips.

Darcy giggled, her sparkling blue eyes meeting his with as much lust and heat as he could feel throughout his body.

"And what do you want me to do... Sir?" she asked as she looked up at him and gave him a smile.

He could tell she was trying to hold back a giggle. Hades looked into her eyes, and the question made him feel on edge. He wasn't entirely sure how to answer. Each moment, each sound, each touch was like an undiscovered territory.

No one had ever asked him, in this sense, what he wanted.

Even his former partners.

Tenille took what she wanted, albeit, he gave it freely because he trusted her to uphold his boundaries and limits, which she did.

Persephone had never once asked him what he wanted in all the time they'd been together. He'd been more than giving, always romancing her, trying to be everything he thought she wanted, and it had worked for a long time. But the way in which Darcy asked him the question left him, for the first time, speechless.

"Hades?" She stopped her motions, her voice bringing him back to the here and now.

He blinked and swallowed. "Yes?"

"Are you okay?" she asked with sweet concern.

"Yes. I am green," he whispered before taking a deep breath to answer her. He'd never said such words aloud before, and the reality of that was not lost on him.

"To answer your question, darling Darcy," he said as he looked deep into her eyes and he ripped off the Band-Aid, his words leaving him feeling a newfound sense of freedom he hadn't known he missed.

"I want you to please me."

CHAPTER TWENTY

I WANT YOU to please me.

Something about the way in which Hades said the words felt heavy.

As if the words themselves were some kind of ancient artifact, some scribbled hieroglyphic prophecy. Like some form of chant or affirmation one would use to manifest their dreams, their desires.

Darcy looked at the sinful god in front of her, his dark eyes, his luscious lips, the perfect tone of his forearms peeking out from his rolled up sleeves.

She could still feel the sting on her flesh where he had smacked her, could feel every time his cock throbbed through his tight, sexy jeans. But most of all, she could feel the levity of those words, the trust in them, and Darcy knew she would oblige.

She would do her best to please this man, no matter what.

Darcy tugged at his jeans once more, and this time Hades let her pull them down while freeing his cock in one fell swoop under the blanket. She made a point of looking in his eyes as her hand wrapped around him, stroking him slowly, building a rhythm. His eyes burned back into hers and she could see the fiery blue haze in them once again.

She noted as she slid her hand up and down his shaft, the length was not one she'd encountered before, and she silently wondered if she should abort her plans altogether, wondering if going down on the sexy god would put her in an early grave. She decided that if this was how she was going to die, it was a damn good way to go.

Hades ran his fingers over her ass once more, right along her seam. He dragged his fingers along her hip, sliding them through the side of her thong, finding her sensitive center, which was quite wet from their torturous explorations.

"Hades..." She let out a strangled sound as he slid a finger into her aching loins. The sudden invasion left her feeling lightheaded and she grabbed him much harder than she'd wanted to, but he did not seem to mind.

His lips traced lines of fire along her neck and she could not help as she thrust her hips against his fingers, feeling the beginning of her own release on the horizon. And just as soon as it had entered her, he slid his fingers slowly out, his eyes never leaving hers.

She watched as he brought his index finger up to his lips, sticking it in his mouth, his tongue licking at it like one licks frosting they've commandeered from a cupcake.

"Mmmm. Tastes just as divine as I remember," he said as he crushed his lips to hers.

Darcy moaned against his lips, unable

to keep her ecstasy bottled up, especially when Hades forced his tongue in her mouth, when she could taste the remnants of herself on his lips. The feelings coursing through her collided with her own memories of just how good his lip service was. How he'd brought her to orgasm with just his tongue alone, and the combination of everything converged on Darcy as she pulled him closer, needing to feel his touch.

"Please, don't stop," she whispered in his ear.

Hades thrust against her hand and she could feel the beginning of wetness seeping out of him as he did so.

He smacked her ass once more, the sting from his palm causing her loins to quiver from the contact.

"Please, don't stop, Sir," he whispered darkly against her ear.

Darcy took a deep breath before repeating the words. "Please, don't stop, Sir."

Hades slid his hand softly over the spot he'd smacked, rubbing gently before dragging his hand over her hip once more, fingers finding her entrance again, his lips claiming hers, muffling her moans of ecstasy with his mouth.

Darcy thrust her hips forward against his hand while she built up her own rhythm around his cock, and it did not take long for him to bring her to completion. Hades slid a second finger inside her walls, curling it just so.

"Hades..." she moaned against his lips as her insides pulsed around him.

When he slid his fingers out, she did not waste another moment as she slid beneath the blanket, replacing her hand with her mouth. The sound that escaped his throat was surprising. He grabbed her by the back of her hair, thrusting up into her mouth with an aggression that told her he was not far off from his own orgasm.

Darcy circled her tongue around the head of his cock, using her right hand to hold him at the base, her left to massage his balls. Hades picked up his pace, quickening his rhythm as he tightened his fingers in her hair to the point it stung.

The Earth felt as if it was trembling beneath them as he released himself down her throat, his head falling back, mouth slack.

Darcy swallowed the taste of him down,

noting that it actually tasted... sweet.

Like sweet cream in bitter, black coffee.

She could hear the ending of Chucky approaching as she came up from her coveted spot underneath the blanket, just as Hades seemed to be regaining his senses. She could hear the faint sound of a zipper as she turned herself around, pulling her knees up to her chest as he situated himself once more. When she felt an arm wrap around her, his head brushing against her back, the sounds of his labored breathing in her ears, she couldn't help but smile.

CHAPTER TWENTY-ONE

IT WAS AS if their moment in the park had set free an animal Hades could not remember stowing. Yet, now that the beast was unleashed from within, he did not want to cage it anymore.

His entire body felt alive, every nerve, every synapse, every beat of his immortal heart felt fresh, invigorating, new. It was an addicting sort of feeling.

Which was why when he'd swept Darcy off the park lawn and transported her home to her apartment, he knew he should take it easy.

Too much of anything could be bad, but for the moment he did not care.

So he followed Darcy into her apartment, locked the door, and did not waste time dilly-dallying.

His hands rushed over her body, down her arms, around her waist, fingers sliding up her thighs under her dress, over the soft flesh of her ass, which made his cock twitch.

"Hades..." she purred as her own hands started to work at the buttons of his shirt.

"Yes?" he said as his fingers slid up the back of her dress, angling to find her zipper.

His head was swimming as a million thoughts and feelings assaulted him. Thoughts of how much he wanted this.

How much he wanted her.

Her fingers roamed over the expanse of his chest as she pushed his shirtsleeves down. She looked up at him with deep blue eyes that reminded him of the pristine waters of the Mediterranean Sea.

"What is it?" he asked as he tried to regain his breath.

Perhaps, I've miscalculated.

Perhaps, she does not want this...

"Nothing, I just...umm..."

Hades could feel panic starting to form in his chest.

He watched as Darcy blushed, averting his gaze, and a smile formed on her lips.

"I mean drunk or in the dark is one thing, but now... here... I just ummm... you're really sexy, do you know that? Of course you know that, you have to know that, and like, I mean this is... umm... like..." she started to ramble. A soft smile tugged at his lips.

He found it rather adorable when she got so flustered she couldn't speak.

"I would not call myself sexy, but it pleases me to know that you find me attractive," he said honestly as he pulled her against him.

"Yes, definitely..." she said with a deep breath. "I just... feel things when I'm with you. Things I don't normally feel. You make me feel like I'm flying, like I can do anything, be anything I want..." She leaned closer, her lips dancing against his as she closed the distance between them.

He broke apart from her and in her eyes, he felt more naked than he'd ever felt in his long life.

"You make me feel things, too, Darcy. Things I didn't think I could feel again... and..." He leaned his forehead against hers as his fingers pulled at her zipper slowly. "It's a lot to feel sometimes, but it feels..."

Darcy's eyes were full of fire as they stared back at him, and Hades knew he had become Icarus once again. And though he had lived centuries swearing he'd never let himself come close enough to being burned again, he knew without a doubt that he wanted to burn in Darcy's golden light. He wanted to let her consume him, and the realization was both startling and frightening.

"It feels so fucking good," he breathed against her lips, and she shimmied out of her dress, her fingers slowly working at his belt, the buttons of his jeans.

"I don't want that feeling to go away," she said as she pushed his jeans and boxers down. The soft sound of them crumpling to the floor, the jingle of his belt buckle hitting the hardwood echoed in the space between them as he stepped out of them.

He stood naked before her, and could not help but feel like a moth emerging from a cocooned slumber as he looked at her with trepidation and awe.

Mate.

The Diviner had shown him the truth, and there was no fighting it, no denying it. For when he looked at her, he knew nothing had ever been more true.

"Darling Darcy..." He ran his hands through her hair, over her shoulders. "I am not going anywhere... not tonight."

Not ever.

Desire flooded his body, from his head to his toes, and everything was a beautiful, dark blur as they made their way across the living room, stumbling through Darcy's bedroom door, fighting at each other's last remains of clothing, racing against the clock like there was no tomorrow.

And for Hades, there was no tomorrow.

There was only this moment, this one perfect moment.

There was only Darcy, and the maddening desire that burned throughout his entire being, causing his flames to catch once more.

Darcy's bra fell to the floor in an instant, her pert, hardened nipples brushing against his chest sending a shock wave directly to his cock.

"Where are you, Darcy?" he asked shakily, needing to hear her say the words.

Everything with Darcy felt like a dream. A dream Hades worried he'd wake up from, once again alone and back in Hell. As if he'd imagined every curve, every scent, every feeling.

"Very, very fucking green, Sir."

Hades's lips turned up into a delicious smile as they trailed down her collarbone, over her breasts. He pulled a nipple into his mouth, sucking slowly, his tongue brushing her soft flesh. Darcy's head fell back in ecstasy as she fell against the unmade bed.

"You remember your words?" he breathed the words against her flesh and did not miss the goosebumps that rose as he did so. The sight made him feel powerful in a way he'd never felt before, knowing that just his words, his touch could do such things to this beautiful mortal who had somehow captivated him.

Who'd brought him back to life.

'Green, yellow, and Mushu," she panted.

"Good girl," he said, feeling emblazoned by the display of her before him. Her dark hair fell around her shoulders, her blue eyes alive with fire that echoed the color of his flames.

Darcy dug her fingers into the side of Hades's hips, pulling him close as she wrapped her legs around him. The motion sent a wave of panic through him that he did not expect. The sight of her beneath him stirred memories and emotions in him he hadn't felt in so long. Thoughts of sinking himself inside of her, of her hands wrapped around his wrists, of giving her the one thing he held onto with all his might. The power to rule him.

Hades's body locked at the thought, the realization as the anxiety spread. He needed to get a hold of himself or he'd lose control of the moment. So, as Darcy's hands slid over his bare ass, he did not think twice about turning her around, about forcing her up against the edge of the bed, where she couldn't touch him, where she couldn't take anything from him.

Not yet.

Hades felt a surge of energy, of relief

flood his system as Darcy let out a soft sound from his force, and his fingers hooked into the sides of her thong. A wave of energy coursed through him and he did not hesitate, did not try to control it.

Instead, he let it fill him up and embraced it.

Hades pulled at her panties, hard enough that he snapped the straps, and let them fall to the floor.

Darcy turned her head to peer over her shoulder, her gaze taking in the sight of him.

Hades slid his knee between her legs, pushing them apart as he leaned over her, running his hand down her spine until he stopped at her ass once more.

"Didn't expect you to be such an ass man, but I'm not complaining," Darcy said with a giggle.

Hades let his palm smack her flesh, watching how it jiggled, watched as her fair flesh turned pink where he'd laid his hand, and she giggled once more. The sound was both somehow sweet and sexy at the same time, and a smile spread across his face.

His arms circled her, his left hand cupping her breast from behind, fingers pulling and tugging at her nipples as his right hand traveled down her abdomen, slowly teasing her once more, feeling her soaked entrance.

Darcy pushed back against him.

"Not yet, darling."

"Please..." she begged as she arched her back, her fingernails seeking purchase in her sheets.

"Please, what?" he growled in her ear,

bringing her flush with his aching cock against her ass.

"Please, Sir... I... I don't know how much longer I can stand this," she panted, and he could feel the intensity of her arousal, her energy reaching a new high.

Darcy let out a sigh of ecstasy, and his right hand held her by the throat, tilting her head back to get a good look at her. Her bright eyes were filled with lust, with awe, and... love.

Hades stilled as realization overcame him.

Love.

The word was like a curse being lifted, like a caged spirit finding its freedom.

Memories of Persephone flashed in his brain; of stolen kisses, of long days and nights spent in their own little corner of

Heaven built in an idyllic Hell. Of the way she'd run her fingers through his long dark hair, of smiles and flowers that grew in the darkest of places.

He'd known love because of her, but now...

Now, he knew love again because of the woman he held in his arms. His heart thudded loudly in his chest.

Hades let his fingers travel down her abdomen, dipping below through her wet, slick folds, feeling her arousal. He slowly pushed his fingers in and out of her, her insides pulsing as he did so. Slowly, he drew them back out, sliding them along her ass, spreading the wetness as best he could. Gently, he pushed one finger into her ass and Darcy immediately tensed.

"Where are you?" he asked in a husky

voice.

"Green..." Darcy groaned as she pushed herself back on his fingers.

"Are you ready for me, darling?" Hades's cock throbbed against her ass.

Darcy breathed deeply, the sound of her pants filling the air like sweet music.

"Yes, Sir," she said the words, and Hades could hear the desperation in them, but even if he couldn't, he would not have missed the waves of heightened energy emanating from her. So he did not think twice, did not hesitate as he lined himself up, pushing himself into Darcy without haste.

The sound that escaped her throat was the most pleasant sound he'd ever heard as he speared her, feeling the warm tightness wrapped around his cock. His fingers tightened around her neck, and he closed his eyes in ecstasy as a feeling he hadn't felt in ages overcame him. The words came without warning out of his mouth. His other hand slid over her front, pulling her back against him so she was flush to his body and he was as deep as he could go.

"Mine," he growled darkly.

"Yes, Sir," Darcy whispered softly as his hands made their way down her arms, fingers intertwining with hers as he pushed her forward, bracing her against the bed. Hades closed his eyes, leaning his head against her back, his flames igniting all around him, around her.

She was warm and wet, and it had been so long since he'd been inside of anyone, let alone someone he loved.

Centuries, even.

Hades's muscles tensed, and he stilled, afraid to move.

Afraid that the walls would come crumbling down around them.

"Gods, you feel so fucking good..." he moaned as the scent of coconut and vanilla filled his senses and he buried his face in her hair. He slowly started to move his hips, building a torturous rhythm as she relaxed in his hold.

"Hades..." Darcy moaned into the sheets, her voice strained. "I'm so close..." Her fingers tightened in the sheets beneath his hands.

"Say my name again," he growled in her ear as he pulled out, only to thrust in deeper, causing Darcy to let out a startled yelp. When his fingers found her soaked pussy once more, resistance was futile, and it only fueled his desire more as he moved them in tandem to his thrusts, his thumb brushing against her sensitive clit as the sound of his skin slapping against hers sounded in the air, amidst her whimpers and moans.

Her pleasure was his, and his alone.

"Oh, Hades..." she groaned, her voice strained and full of lust.

"Louder," he growled once more as he took her earlobe in his mouth, biting gently as Darcy let out a soft cry of pleasure. Hades commanded her once more as a wave of energy coursed through him, sliding out of her ass once more only to slam into her harder, faster than the last. He could feel as her legs buckled slightly from the force of him against her, but he persisted.

He needed more.

He wanted to feel her come around him, wanted to fill her as he exploded into a million pieces, only to be put back together again by her touch, her lips, her voice, the feel of her in his arms.

"Hades." Her voice went up an octave, but it was still far too quiet. He wanted the whole town, the whole world to know she was his.

Hades pulled his hands from her, tangling his fingers in her hair, twisting it around his wrist as he pulled, forcing her neck to turn and look up at him while his other hand found her ass once more.

He let out a crisp smack, watching the expression on her face as she winced slightly.

"I said louder, darling," he breathed out

as he crushed his lips to hers, his thrusts coming faster as he chased his pleasure. "Darcy..."

"Fucking hell... Hades!" Darcy screamed as she came, her body tensing, tightening around his cock as he stilled, riding out his orgasm as he spilled himself into her.

The room rattled and shook, tiny trinkets and books falling from their shelves around them like rain.

Hades pulled Darcy back against him, burying his face in her hair as emotion overcame him.

It seemed like hours until they moved apart. Darcy sat up, and Hades missed her warmth but followed suit.

"Well, I should um... get cleaned up," Darcy said as she cleared her throat, a blush creeping onto her cheeks once more.

Hades could not deny the sight stirred forgotten feelings, thoughts. He took a step closer to Darcy and she did not shy away.

"Where is your bathroom?" he asked, his breaths still edging on the verge of panting as he had not quite recovered yet.

"Umm, through there," Darcy said pointing to a small sliver of doorway adjacent to her bedroom.

Hades ran his fingers through her hair softly, letting his fingertips leave tiny trails along her cheek.

"Let me." He spoke softly as he drew his lips to hers.

Darcy nodded in response.

Hades took his time in the small bathroom as he drew a warm bath for her, and he noted her eyes were filled with many emotions. Some, he'd recognized, but others a mystery. He took in the sight of her naked before him still, noting the beginnings of slight bruises, the markings on her neck where'd he sucked, nibbled, and bit at her skin in the throes of his desires.

He pulled her by the hand toward the tub, and as she stepped in, he felt awash with emotions, his stomach turning from the sight of his markings, but his heart strangely full. Because even though a part of him hated to see the remains of where he'd touched her, a part of him relished the sight.

He'd touched the sun, and the remainder was all over her perfect flesh.

He quietly helped her into the tub, and sudden anxiety flooded him. A part of him worried perhaps she may need space to process everything that had just happened between them, but another part of him did not want to leave her side, wanted to crawl behind her in the tiny tub and hold her close.

"Are you okay?" she whispered, breaking him from his spell.

Hades shook his head as he looked down at her.

"You are asking me if I am okay?" he asked softly. "I should be asking you that question..."

"I'm okay," she said as her gaze caught his, and he could not fight it. He found himself crawling in the tub behind her.

As they both came down from the euphoria of only moments ago, Darcy leaned against him and Hades wrapped his arms around her, trailing warm water up and down her body. His fingers gently massaged the shower gel into her skin, softly ran through her hair as he placed the softest kiss on her neck.

Darcy's eyes fluttered shut. She reached her arm up behind her, her fingers tracing his lips as her eyes settled on his.

"I'm better than okay," she said with a smirk. Hades could not help his lips tugging into a soft smile.

Darcy let her free hand fall over the back of his as he held her close. It wasn't the first time Hades had experienced aftercare, he'd been held many times by Tenille after particularly trying scenes. Yet, it was the first time he'd ever given it, and as he held Darcy in his arms with only the desire to care and nurture her, Hades could not deny his heart felt full, and he wished the night would last forever.

***

The sun shone through Darcy's window, the beam of light falling on her like she was an angel from the heavens. Hades took a moment to gaze upon her, noticing all the little details that were so much more pronounced now.

How thick and full her eyelashes were, set against her fair complexion.

How the sunlight lit up her dark locks, making little strands look like copper and gold.

Or the curve of that spot where her neck met her shoulder, where his lips had left marks upon her skin that she would surely have to cover up with makeup.

Hades knew as he reached out, softly

running his fingers over her silky hair, that the dam within him was broken. His heart beat loudly in his chest, his entire being swelling with an emotion he thought he'd lost. He'd bared his weakness and his demons, to this mortal woman and that frightened him more than he wanted to admit.

He'd let her in.

He'd let her into a place within him that was dark and cold, a place not even Tenille was permitted to go.

He'd let her into his heart.

But despite this revelation, despite the vulnerability that he felt in this very moment, he knew that even it could not last forever.

Reality was here to take him home, and for the first time in a long time, he did not want to go home.

He wanted to stay on the surface, gorge on tacos from Taco Tim's, and watch scary movies in the park at dusk. He wanted to wake up next to this beautiful woman who tasted like milk and honey, who had somehow found a way through his impenetrable walls. He wanted to make her frozen drinks with tiny umbrellas, and he wanted to kiss her until he couldn't breathe. He wanted to live in her arms, in her bed until he forgot about everything and anything else.

Darcy stirred at his touch, and he found himself in sorrow. Each second he was one step closer to breaking this perfect bubble.

"Good morning." She smiled, the sun lighting up her blue eyes like diamonds. She pulled the covers up to hide her mouth, her eyes still bright and full of life. Hades had never seen anything quite so beautiful.

"Good morning, darling," he whispered, taking in the sight of her.

"You stayed..." she said as she pulled herself closer to him, ruffling the flower printed sheets against him.

"You were very persuasive," he said with a wicked grin. Darcy let out a laugh, and he thought the sound was the sweetest thing he'd ever heard.

"When will you be back?" she asked as her smile faded.

"Not for a while."

"What's a while? A couple weeks? A month?" Darcy's fingers traced lines along his jaw, her eyes fixated on his lips.

"Three months. I likely won't be back

until after the New Year."

"Likely?" she said shakily.

"It depends on work," he said as he ran his fingers through her hair softly.

"Aren't you like the god of the Underworld? Can't you just do whatever you want?" she pined.

Hades let out a soft chuckle.

"I am one god in the Underworld. Not the only one. Though, most people don't realize there are other gods who reside there, so I understand the confusion. But no, I cannot do whatever I want. I have a job to uphold. The souls that come through to me need to be categorized, sorted, ferried to the eternal resting places. Death waits for no one."

Darcy frowned, and he hated the sight.

"My time needs to be cleared by

Lucifer," he said as he let his fingers trail over the soft flesh of her neck, over the pronounced pink hickeys left from the previous night.

After arriving back at the apartment, Hades found it rather difficult to keep his hands or his lips to himself. The orgasm he'd felt at the park had left him with fresh desire, ignited his fire once more, and he needed to burn through it. He needed to burn through every bit of Darcy until he'd consumed her in his flames.

The realization overcame him, and it was exciting and frightening all at once. Perhaps, even though he did not want to distance himself from her at all, it was probably a wise idea. He needed some clarity, for, in Darcy's presence, he could not think straight.

"Oh, okay," she said as she bit her lip. Hades could tell she wanted to say more, and he could feel her anxiety invading their bubble.

"You will be the first to know of my surface plans," he said with a half smile, trying to reassure her.

"Right. Yeah. Of course." She smiled back, though Hades did not believe for a second it was genuine, it was much easier for him to believe it was.

CHAPTER TWENTY-TWO

IT WAS QUITE a rainy day in Los Angeles, but Darcy couldn't stop smiling. Despite there being no sun anywhere in sight, Darcy could not shake the warmth that spread through her being.

She skipped through the puddles, feeling a new sense of confidence that hadn't existed within her before. And when the barista at Starbucks wrote Darby on her cup, she didn't even care.

Waking up next to the god—no, the man—she had thought was certainly a dream, Darcy realized two things. The first, was that she was alive, and he was really in her apartment, in her bed. She hadn't imagined the whole thing. The second, was that as she looked at him in the cascading sunlight, she felt closer to him than she'd ever felt to anyone in her entire life, and the way he looked at her…

She knew the Diviner was right.

They were meant to be together.

Soul mates.

Divided across realms, brought together by serendipity. Though the morning had been bittersweet, as much as she'd loved gazing into his dark brown eyes, she knew she could not keep him locked in her apartment like a sexy prisoner forever.

Though, I wouldn't mind being locked up with him for an eternity if last night was any indication...

Her mind turned the memory over and over, as if it alone were afraid something could wipe it away.

The memory of his touch, how he held her.

How his touch bordered on pain and pleasure that left her feeling a mixture of emotions.

How he'd filled her and then some, making it seem as if she'd tear in half from the force of his cock, which she could feel deep within her spine from every thrust.

She longed for more.

More of his touch.

It was as if his touch would never be enough.

When Darcy finally settled in at her desk with her Cafe Mocha with extra whip cream, Sandy, Patrick, and Cate were all waiting in the lobby.

"Good afternoon, y'all," Darcy said, looking back and forth between them all.

"Afternoon, Darcy," Cate said, squinting her eyes at her suspiciously.

"Everything okay?" Darcy asked as she straightened her space in front of her.

"Cate's been trying to get ahold of you," Sandy whispered.

Darcy looked up into the dual-toned eyes of the stone-faced goddess, who was still eyeing her very suspiciously.

Did I do something wrong?

"There was a small earthquake last

night. Right around your area," Cate said as she raised an eyebrow.

"What?" Darcy's eyes shot up in alarm. She didn't remember the earthquake… only a few things falling from her shelves, likely from the shaking floors during her tryst with Hades. She hated how weak the flooring was in her apartment. If one jumped too hard, the photo frames would fall over on her bookshelf.

"Mhmmm. Small tremor, but nonetheless, it knocked out some power lines." Cate's voice carried an air of suspicion that matched her eyes.

Darcy suddenly felt very on the spot.

"Oh, ummm, well, that sucks. I didn't feel anything, though," she said as she took a long sip of her coffee.

Cate did not break her gaze. "I'm glad

you're okay."

"Yup, yup. Right as rain." She smiled, wanting nothing more than to escape the impenetrable gaze of Hecate herself.

Just as Cate was about to speak, the door opened and Gunner slid in with a box of doughnuts.

Saved by the shifter, thank God.

"What's this?" Cate asked as she used one finger to open the box. Gunner attempted to shut it on her hand, but the look in Cate's eyes was not one to be trifled with.

What is her deal this afternoon?

"Thought you guys might appreciate some sugar on this shitty day." He shrugged as he set the box down on the counter.

"Well, you don't have to tell me twice,"

Sandy said as she pushed past Patrick and dived in for the bright pink frosted doughnut.

Cate crossed her arms and sighed. "This doesn't make up for not telling me about your little... excursion," she grumbled.

Gunner cast her a look Darcy could only describe as full of heat.

"Maybe not, but a little sugar never hurt anyone," he said with a wicked smile. "Not to mention, there's plenty more begging involved, but that—" he said as he sauntered closer to her, wrapping his arm around her waist.

Darcy watched Cate jump nearly two inches off the floor at the public display, her cheeks actually reddening. She moved to push Gunner off, but he only tightened his grip, his whispering something in her ear that made her eyes widen.

Cate relented as she pushed him off, her gaze catching Darcy's. "This discussion isn't over." She grabbed a doughnut and stormed out of the rescue with Gunner, who was wearing a sly grin on his face. He pointed at Darcy.

"You can thank me later, Dani," he said with a chuckle.

"It's Darcy," she said, feeling rather self-conscious for the moment.

CHAPTER TWENTY-THREE

HADES WALKED THROUGH the door to see Meg at her desk reading a book. She twirled her long copper locks, never bringing her eyes up to even acknowledge he had arrived.

"Good afternoon, Meg," he grumbled.

"Uh-huh. Afternoon, Sir."

Hades huffed, feeling already

melancholy enough that he did not wish to fight with the woman. Instead, he looked down to see what had her so captivated.

12 Hunks of Herculeia by C. Rochelle.

Hades raised an eyebrow at his secretary, noting the waves of energy flowing off her were full of desire.

"Really, Meg? I would have thought you'd be more of a crime thriller person." He crossed his arms, finally gaining her attention.

She only smirked back at him.

"Since when do you take interest in anything I do?" she teased him.

"You are my employee, I take interest in whether or not you do your job."

"I can read a book while I work." She waved him off.

Hades rolled his eyes, pulling the book

from her grasp, intrigued for the moment what had her so worked up. The words that he scanned left a blush creeping up his neck and he soon slammed the book back down, looking away from Meg, who wore a wide smile on her face.

"Carry on," he said as he cleared his throat.

"Mhmm. Serves you right," she said, popping off her gum.

Hades straightened his shoulders and headed for the door to his office.

"By the way, Sir... you have a visitor. He's been here for an hour, so I wouldn't keep him waiting much longer if I were you," Meg said with a wicked grin.

Panic surged through Hades as he wondered who it could be. It wasn't like him to get many visitors. Truthfully, the only visitors the man had were his sisters, Hera and Demi.

Hades pushed open his door, shutting it quickly as he entered his office. His blood chilled as he looked at the guest sitting on his couch, long arms extended along the backside. A small collection of papers sat in his lap, and the expression on his face was one Hades had seen all too many times.

Intrigue.

"Hello, Hades."

"Hello, Lucifer," Hades grumbled as he stalked to his desk.

"You've been kicking up quite a fuss lately, haven't you?" The fallen angel smirked at him.

"I don't know what you are talking about," Hades said as he sank into his chair, turning on his computer.

"Well, for starters. I see the band has gotten back together." He laughed.

"What?"

"Hades & Hecate, ride or die besties for life," Lucifer mocked with a laugh. "I do hope the poor shifter had a more favorable outcome than what Cate is usually known for." He narrowed his eyes.

"Um, as far as I know, yes. He's just fine." Hades checked his email but still did not see an approval for the Archives request.

"You aren't going to find your request there," Lucifer said, grasping his small stack of papers as he leaned forward, rising from the couch.

He walked closer to Hades, pulling his gaze from the computer.

"What request?" Hades swallowed nervously.

"What reason do you have for needing to make a trip to the Archives, hmm?" Lucifer stood against Hades's desk, looking as menacing as ever, but such a stance did not frighten Hades.

"I would like to do some... research, that's all." Hades kept his tone even.

"What kind of research?"

"We have a Diviner. I'd like to take a look at it."

Lucifer pursed his lips. "Would this have anything to do with Cate and the shifter?"

"Yes." Hades did not think twice about lying to his friend, his boss. It should have bothered him, but yet, he could not give up Orion. The man had come to him for help, and against his better judgment, he'd obliged. He was not about to sell out Orion and Trinity. After all, they had put their trust in him.

"Very well, then." Lucifer slid him a piece of paper with a large "Approve" stamp beaming at him.

Hades noted he still held two pieces of paper.

"Aphrodite called me yesterday. Said you made an appearance at the DeLux, demanding she give you the list to Wednesday night's speed dating event. Is this true?" he asked calmly.

"Yes, but I—"

"Hades, Hades, Hades. How out of character for you." Lucifer snickered.

"Always so controlled, so calm and collected. Who has your panties in a bunch, dear Hades? Do not leave out any sordid details." He smiled devilishly.

"It's not like that. I—"

"It's the girl from the van, isn't it? What was her name again... Delilah... Delores... D..."

"Darcy."

"Ah yes, Darcy. Cate's friend." Lucifer's eyes sparkled with interest. The man loved a good secret, good gossip. He'd lord such things over you to get what he wanted. It was his way of business. Hades hated divulging the truth to him, but Lucifer knew him almost as well as Cate. There truly was not much he could hide from the man, at least in the areas of his personal life.

"Yes."

"That's why you went to Aphrodite, isn't

it. You don't want Cate to know your feelings for her dear, dear mortal friend."

Hades did not answer.

"Little." Lucifer tossed the paper on the desk, and it fell atop the Archive approval sheet. "Darcy Little. That is her name."

"Why are you telling me confidential information?" Hades asked, still feeling wary about which way Lucifer was leaning with this sudden influx of information he was offering.

"I came as soon as Aphrodite called. Imagine my shock when the ever punctual god, who I can always count on being where he should, was not available. I checked my calendar, I knew you were due back here. But yet... you were not here. Hera had not heard from you, Demi said she saw you, that you came back early.

But you were nowhere to be found. Even a scan through the Underworld's private security cameras would not produce you. You went back to the surface to see Aphrodite, but when she did not give you what you wanted you stayed. And I figured it out. You stayed on the surface because you wanted to see her. Darcy. Like a moth to a flame, Hades. All these centuries and you are still just a hopeless romantic, aren't you?"

Lucifer played with the last piece of paper in his hand.

Hades did not answer, for he could not. What could he say? So instead he asked the only question he could think of.

"What's the last paper?"

"Oh, this?" Lucifer said as he set down the paper on top of the list that highlighted

Darcy's name. "This, I'm afraid, is the bad news."

Hades sighed. "What is the bad news?"

"You will have to pay for the damages to the Den Of Sin, respectably."

"Damages?" Hades's voice rose.

"Yes, apparently your little quake caused some malfunctioning of certain equipment. A chandelier was broken." Lucifer smiled deviously.

"Oh for fuck's sake, it was an accident," Hades huffed. "Why are you smiling?"

"Because it appears, even after all these years, you are not perfect, Hades. You still crack just like the rest of us."

Hades grabbed the sheet from Lucifer's hands, scribbling his name down quickly.

"Done. Can I get back to work now?"

"I'd appreciate that. Also, no more

playing hooky. Your time off ceases until your next seasonal outing," Lucifer said with a smile as he walked out of Hades's office.

"Fuck," he groaned, knowing the next few months were going to be absolute hell.

***

Hades walked up to the towering silver warehouse set amidst the red soil and cacti like some spaceship from a Science Fiction drive-in movie. The barren landscape was both somehow threatening and non-threatening. Though it appeared no one was around Hell's Archives for miles, Hades knew the security was top of the line around the perimeter, which was why he had opted to go in alone through the front, while Orion and Trinity would infiltrate from elsewhere.

The catacombs that once acted as an underground passageway during the original war with Heaven were still very much accessible, but no one aside from Hades, Lucifer, and the original Fallens knew about the access point. Though Hades would never divulge he'd found out about them only after discovering Lucifer using them many moons ago when he was... entertaining himself.

Hades swiped his Reaper Row badge against the sleek building, noting that he did not feel as nervous as he probably should have. But then again, that may have been due to the excess of energy running through his body. Since his date with Darcy, he'd felt rather confident, joyous even, in his day-to-day life. Though he wished he could contact her, tell her how he missed her, how he thought of her almost daily, he knew he'd have to wait until he was cleared to be able to speak with her again.

Cell reception just didn't cross realms, even though the crossroads demons had been begging for such things for years now.

While security on the outside of the Archives was to be expected, security on the inside of the building was minimal, at best. After all, the building was designed to keep the artifacts, curses, and magical entities in the building.

It did not take Hades long to find the hallway that led to the old catacombs. He looked both ways, making sure the coast was clear before he opened the door, closing it quietly. Kneeling down to the floor, he searched for the latch in the floorboards that would lead to the trap door that went down straight from the hallway into the catacombs, which would come out on the other side of Hell all the way by ButterNut Bakery.

Orion and Trinity stood in the shadows looking a little worse for wear. Trinity clung to Orion like a second skin, and Hades did not miss the way Orion held the woman close, like he was afraid she'd disappear if he did otherwise.

The sight made his own heart flutter in longing. It had only been days since he'd seen Darcy, since he'd explored the curves of her body, felt her heartbeat beneath his palm as his hands traced their way up her chest, her neck.

Since he'd felt utter bliss for the first

time in centuries.

"Come on, let's get this show on the road." Hades sighed.

The Archives were not much more than a warded, protected warehouse full of old dusty artifacts. Still, Hades could not help his own curiosity as he walked through the shadowed halls, searching the shelves for the Diviner that was listed in the Archives's logs.

Orion and Trinity searched the shelves in front of him, and although he knew he should stay near to them, curiosity bloomed in his stomach. His gaze settled on the identification numbers, I89 in front of him. The Diviner in the system had been logged as I100. He looked back and forth, watching as Orion pulled down a large stone slab from a high shelf. Trinity watched from below, chewing on her fingernails as Orion brought the tablet down.

"I think this is it," Orion said shakily. Trinity came up closer, looking over his arm at the grey, cobwebbed tablet.

Hades looked over as well, noting the language written on it was one that was rather ancient.

Ancient Angelic, to be accurate.

What the hell is an angel tablet doing in Hell's Archives?

Orion ran his fingers over the indentations, whispering the ancient language even Hades didn't speak.

Of course, Orion would be able to understand the language. He was part angel, after all, well versed in much of the ancient languages as a liaison between

Heaven and Hell.

But it was the small, crisp, sweet voice that he did not expect.

Trinity spoke.

Her voice was clear as a bell, and Hades watched as Orion turned to her, shock and awe in his eyes.

"Say that again..." Orion said as he swallowed.

Trinity's eyes widened as she looked up at Orion. "Y... You... can... hear me?"

Orion let out a laugh. "Yeah, baby. I can hear you..." he said with a smile.

Hades looked away, feeling as if he was watching something he had no business watching. The joy in Trinity's eyes was apparent as they filled with tears, and Orion pulled her close with one arm.

"I can hear you..." he said as he closed

his eyes while Trinity ran her fingers over the tablet.

Hades slid his hands in his pocket as he headed for 1100.

Soon enough, they'd have to put everything back as they found it, and make their way back to the catacombs, to try and make it as if they'd never been there at all. But Hades did not want to leave without finding out all he could about the Diviner, about the ancient shifters artifact that predicted... mates.

Gunner had claimed it predicted his connection to Cate, and though Hades did not have any evidence to prove such a thing was true, he could only rely on the feeling, the magic he'd felt when both he and Darcy touched the artifact.

The way it felt as if every path led

directly to wherever she was.

Even now, as he set his gaze on the small moonstone rock in the Archives, he could feel the magic, the labyrinthine lines that would undoubtedly lead him to her.

Hades plucked the moonstone from its shelf, turning it just so that, in the low light of the Archives, it shimmered almost as if it were underwater.

A loud bang from across the hallway alerted him as his hand closed around the moonstone. He quietly approached the sound of the bang, noting the sparks that flew as if something metal had collided with the shelves, with an ancient artifact.

Gold sparks erupted, and Hades instantly felt panicked as he saw the looming shadow of a winged creature that most certainly should not be in Hell's

Archives.

An angel.

What the fuck is an angel doing in Hell's Archives?

Anxiety flooded him as he realized the shadow of the angel was headed in the direction of Orion and Trinity.

Hades didn't think, he just acted.

It was almost as if he could feel the ominous angelic presence's rage, could feel its desperation, its need to put an end to whatever it was that called it to the Archives in the first place.

"Hey!" Hades shouted, trying to gain the angel's attention.

The shadow turned in his direction, and through the slivers of cracks in the wire shelves of the Archives, he could see Orion and Trinity as they locked eyes with him.

HADES

If he could distract the angel, perhaps they'd have a chance to leave the way they came, the angel none the wiser.

Hades nodded to Orion, a silent understanding passing between them, and as the angel turned the corner, Hades closed his eyes knowing there was no way out of this situation that was favorable. But he was not about to let Orion and Trinity take the fall. He'd agreed to help them, after all.

Hades stood his ground, blue flames catching all along his skin, the edges of his hair, igniting within his deep, dark eyes.

"Well, well, if it isn't Hades... Long time no see..." the angel said with a sneer. He stood tall against the silver walls of the Archives, but there was no reflection except that of his large, almost monstrous white wings that resembled something more sinister than of the soft, feathered variety everyone always attributed. No, instead, these wings were massive and looked more like an ivory version of flying fox wings, a single claw.

Cassiel...

Hades hadn't seen the angel since everything that had transpired back when...

When I gave Persephone her locket and left her on the surface...

"I'd say it's nice to see you, but I'd rather not," Hades said as Cassiel sauntered toward him, his silvery white light radiating around him, his hand grasping his sleek silver blade. He looked every bit the angel of mercy, coming to avenge the wrong. Looks were always deceiving where angels were involved.

"Seems you've been sticking your head in where it does not belong," Cassiel said as he stopped only an inch from Hades's face.

Hades looked the angel up and down. "I have access to this Archive, but you... What in God's name are you doing down here, hmmm? Seems a far drive for one as yourself."

"No farther than the Den Of Sin is for demon sin like you." Cassiel smirked.

"I am not a demon, but you already know that."

"Corrupting the innocent, no soul... fucking with demons and Succubi... Sounds pretty 'demon' to me." Cassiel raised an eyebrow at him.

"I'm flattered you've been keeping tabs

on me, Cassiel." Hades smirked.

"What business do you have with my tablet?"

"Your tablet?" Hades crossed his arms, but he did not miss Cassiel's blade, still primed and ready to strike. His flames did not die down either.

"Yes, my tablet. It has my wards on it, which is why as soon as your demonic fingers touched it, I knew."

"You warded an angel tablet... which you stashed in Hell..." Hades twisted his lips.

"How did you find it? It isn't on the logs," Cassiel asked and Hades could see the panic in his eyes.

"Does it matter?" Hades asked.

"No, I suppose it doesn't. But regardless of how you came across my tablet, the fact is that you did, and that alone puts you in quite a predicament."

"Does it now?"

"Stealing an angel tablet of prophetic knowledge is a crime, Hades." Cassiel smiled.

Prophetic knowledge...

Was Trinity... a prophet?

She had been able to speak, as Orion had hypothesized the damn thing was the key to her doing so, and it appeared he was right. The spell had been broken. She was no longer tongue-tied.

But why had she been in the first place?

What had occurred that caused such a curse?

Did Cassiel have something to do with it?

"We both know I didn't steal anything."

"Yes, we both know that. But it's your word against mine, Hades, and quite frankly, I'm the one with the better reputation."

Cassiel grabbed him by the arm, his fingers gripping Hades tight.

"Hades, you are under Celestial Arrest for possession of an Arcane Celestial Artifact."

There was no turning back, no running now. Hades only hoped that he'd bought Orion and Trinity enough time to escape, and silently cursed himself for not attempting to incinerate the angel in front of him once and for all.

Cassiel's angelic halo extended around Hades, diminishing his flames, and within the blink of an eye, the angel and Hades had disappeared, leaving the Archives empty once more.

CHAPTER TWENTY FOUR

DARCY STARTED TO wonder if she'd imagined it all. If she had somehow dreamed up the delusion of Hades in a fit of loneliness, some on the brink-of-madness type mental breakdown.

For it had been nearly five months since that bittersweet morning she'd woken up to his beautiful, dark eyes gazing back at her like she was the sun, the moon, and the stars.

The marks on her neck had faded, the bruises on her skin had disappeared as if they had never been there, yet, she still could feel them. Somehow, after all this time, despite the fact they did not exist, she could feel them like a living memory.

She could remember the touch, the feel of his fingers around her neck, the warmth of his body pressed against her as he filled her, driving her to the edge of a pleasure she'd never felt in all her life.

He'd looked at her that morning, promising her his return, but it had been almost five months, and Darcy was starting to wonder if, perhaps, she'd been played.

Nothing felt right. Every day felt as if she were in some kind of alternate reality.

The world moved about her as it always had, but somehow it was not the same.

Just as Darcy was about to leave the rescue, the door swung open and Cate stood with a stern look on her face and a canvas tote full of what looked like snacks and...

Is that wine?

"Don't think you're going anywhere this evening. There was a nasty accident up the road by Martin's Flowers. Traffic backed up for miles," Cate said as she hefted the canvas tote onto the desk with a thud.

"What ya got in there? Bricks?" Darcy asked as she pulled at the top of the tote with her pointer finger, peering in.

"Better. I got two bottles of Sangria and dinner."

"And what is dinner?" Darcy asked,

raising an eyebrow.

"Well, for you... sushi. For me... Caprese sandwich on ciabatta. Plus, there was this chocolate cake that I couldn't pass up..."

Darcy smiled softly. "Thanks, boss."

Cate slowly pulled out the items from the bag, glancing at Darcy for a moment before she stopped.

"I thought it might also cheer you up. You've just been kind of... off lately."

Darcy frowned at the words, averting her gaze as she turned away.

"I don't know what you mean," she protested.

Cate continued to set up the food and wine, even pulling out plastic cups.

"I mean, you've had this doe-eyed look on your face for the last month and a half and you think I'm not going to notice?"

Darcy watched Cate twist off the cap to the Sangria, noting the sound of fizz breaking the silence between them. She headed over to the lobby, pulling a chair over toward the desk as Cate pushed a plastic cup toward her along with a container of spicy tuna rolls.

"I..." Darcy paused as Cate sat down in the rolling desk chair. A sudden urge overcame her, one she hadn't quite expected.

It had been a while since Darcy and Cate had a moment alone together. Cate's days had become much more occupied between running the rescue center, and of course, the biggest change in everyone's life—Gunner.

Darcy did not feel jealous, or angry that

the burly shifter had somehow managed to keep Cate satisfied for the last five months. She'd been more than happy that someone was able to get through to Cate. Though, she did miss their serial killer documentaries, weekends spent in Cate's cabin just enjoying each other's company and binging on takeout. Those days were few and far in between now, and Darcy knew who was to blame.

She'd missed telling Cate her secrets, missed poking and prodding the goddess to go out anywhere really.

The unexpected words came out of Darcy's mouth before she took a long drink of her wine from the plastic cup.

"I slept with Hades."

Cate sighed deeply, lifting her gaze to the ceiling.

"I know."

"I didn't mean for it— Wait, did you say you know?" The words hit Darcy a moment too late as she tore open the sushi package.

"Yes," Cate said as she pulled out a foil wrapped package, gingerly opening it to reveal a mouthwatering sandwich.

"How long have you known?"

"A while," Cate said in defeat as she took a bite of her sandwich.

"What's a while?" Darcy could feel the alarms starting to go off in her head.

"I have been friends with Hades for a very long time, Darcy. You think I don't know his appeal? Or his giveaways? I had my suspicions months ago, but I knew the moment that tremor hit near your apartment. When they couldn't figure out where it came from, or what caused it." Cate took a deep breath, setting down her sandwich.

"That had nothing to do with Hades..." Darcy said, swallowing nervously. Cate raised an eyebrow.

"The man has a tendency to cause earthquakes when he gets a little too... excited."

Darcy felt her cheeks redden at the implications.

"I—" she stammered and Cate rolled her eyes. "He said he'd be back but—" Darcy did not finish her sentence. Instead, she poked at a piece of sushi.

"But what?"

"He said he'd be back after the new year, but it's been a while and I'm worried he's not coming back. It's probably just my imagination, maybe I'm over thinking things, but I can't help but feel like maybe something's wrong..." Darcy sighed. "I know I'm probably just being like, a stage five clinger or something, but I thought—"

"For lack of anything else, the man is usually quite punctual when in regard to his surface time," Cate said as she took another bite of her sandwich.

"I can't really explain it. Like I feel this connection. I have ever since we touched the Diviner..."

"You both touched the Diviner?" Cate froze.

"Yeah..."

"And you're still here to tell the story? What exactly happened?" Cate asked coldly.

"Ummm, there were these lines between

us, and like... suddenly, I felt this connection. Like I was being drawn to one place, one person... one..."

"Mate," Cate said the word quietly.

"Yeah. Like a... soulmate, I guess." Darcy had never thought of their connection in such terms, but as she said the words, she found that it left her feeling more content than she'd expected.

Soulmate.

"Soulmate would be an interesting choice of words, given the man has no soul," Cate said dryly.

"What?" Darcy's eyes widened.

What the hell does she mean 'no soul?'

"He gave it up a long time ago. After Persephone left. Said he didn't want to feel, didn't want to remember how any of it felt." Cate set her sandwich down.

"That can't be right. The man I know—"

"The *god* you know," Cate corrected her.

"The god I know is warm and caring, and... I mean, you have to have a soul to be like that right?" Darcy asked aloud, although she was not certain to whom.

"You'd be surprised what you are capable of without a soul," Cate answered.

"It's like ever since we touched the Diviner... when I was with him everything just felt so..."

"Natural." Cate didn't look at Darcy as she spoke.

"Yeah."

"And these last few months, what have you felt?" Cate's voice was serious now.

"Like this ache in my chest, in my being, will never go away. Like I'm stuck in some sort of world that looks and sounds like the one I know is real, but somehow it's not. Like something bad has happened but I can't pinpoint what or where or…" Darcy did not finish and instead, stabbed another piece of sushi with a plastic fork.

"Are you mad?" Darcy asked once she had swallowed down her roll.

"Of course I'm not mad. I'm just… concerned."

"Why? What about the idea of us is so concerning to you?" Darcy did not miss the way in which her voice settled on the word *us*. As if there was an *us* when it came to the two of them. They'd gone out, sure, enjoyed each other's company, and the attraction was nearly palpable between them, but somehow the word felt monumental. They'd never discussed what they were. Hell, everything had happened so fast, it was only a number of days. But somewhere deep in Darcy's being, she knew there was truth in the word. That even though they had not been in contact, even though it all was starting to feel like some dream... That the embers were there, and she could not deny that she wanted more than anything to be an *us*.

Cate sighed as she pulled out her phone, scrolling quietly before answering Darcy.

"I just don't want to see either of you hurt, that's all."

"Who is to say we're going to hurt one another? That's a little presumptuous."

"Where do you see this going, Darcy?" Cate said with a huff.

"What?" The words hit Darcy and her blood chilled.

"Where do you see this... thing... with Hades going? He doesn't spend a ton of time up here, and I know for a fact you'd never be able to survive down in Hell... and I wouldn't want you to."

Of course.

Darcy closed her eyes as understanding befell her.

Persephone.

Cate had mentioned the woman, told her that whatever had transpired between her and Hades had damaged him. She must be the reason for Cate's concern.

"What happened to Persephone?" Darcy asked quietly.

Cate took a long drink of her wine before speaking.

"She left everything to be with him. They'd agreed she'd split her time on the surface, and down below in Hell with him, and for a while, it seemed like the arrangement was working but..."

"What?" Darcy leaned forward, not missing Cate's sorrowful tone.

"It turned out Hell was literally killing her. Despite the fact that she only resided below with him for six months out of the year, the exposure was poisoning her. If they kept their arrangement as they had... Well, she would have died within a year or two."

"Would have?" Darcy's voice was small, and Cate looked at her, her gaze roving over Darcy's expression.

"He let her go. So she could live... and it destroyed him."

Darcy could feel her heart breaking at the admission. "And you think I'm going to do the same?"

"No. I don't. But... waiting around for months—" Cate waved her hand in the air, "—only to see each other for what, a week, at best? You deserve more than that, Darcy."

"I get that there are obstacles, but—"

"But what? You haven't heard from him, right? Walking around in a fog? Second guessing if it's all in your head?" Cate crossed her arms and Darcy could not meet her gaze.

"I know there's got to be a reason!" Darcy huffed. "You yourself said he's usually quite punctual about coming back, and I can't shake this feeling inside that something is wrong, Cate. I just... I know it doesn't make sense. But I also know, without a doubt in my entire being, that there's a damn good reason, but I don't know what I can do to prove it or—"

Cate finished her sandwich, and it was a long moment before she spoke once more.

"Do you love him?" she asked quietly.

Darcy felt rather on the spot at the question, but she answered quickly, not giving much thought to what she already knew to be the truth, despite the fact that it didn't make sense.

"Yes."

Cate sighed. "Then I will look into his sudden... disappearance."

"I want to help..." Darcy offered.

"Of course you do," Cate said as she pulled her phone to her, scrolling as she looked for a number.

"Who are you calling?" Darcy said as

she tried to peer over Cate's shoulder.

"The only person other than myself that knows Hades best," Cate sneered.

"Who is that?"

Cate let out a deep sigh as the phone rang. "The devil himself."

CHAPTER TWENTY-FIVE

HADES WAS CERTAIN of two things; the first, was that Cassiel had taken him somewhere off the books. For Hades had been to Heaven once or twice, and he remembered the crisp, clean scent that filled the clouded paradise, remembered the serene buzzing in his veins upon entering the gates, and the room that

Cassiel was keeping him did not possess either of those qualities.

The second thing Hades was certain of, was that he had been gone far longer than should have been acceptable, which meant that soon enough someone would come looking for him. Though it was his guess as to who would show up first.

Lucifer had been cast out of Heaven ages ago, and thus setting foot anywhere near Heaven or the angels would certainly open old wounds. Then again, if Hades was correct and he was truly outside the confines of Heaven... Well then, Lucifer would have no issues if Hades's celestial prison was, in fact, an earthbound safe house as he suspected.

Despite being dreary and depressing, the room he was being kept in was full of old books and furniture; a rather rickety bed and ill fitting mattress, but it was enough to lay on at least, though it made Hades long for his home that much more. Though the books were not at all anything new, the only book Hades had managed to find any interest in was Pride & Prejudice, which he'd read rather quickly in his early days being kept in his 'celestial prison.'

The room where he resided was old, weathered, and reeked of moss and angel wards. The attendant who brought him meals and guarded his room was, as far as he could tell, mortal, but something about him seemed a bit off the mark for a mortal.

Hades suspected he possessed some kind of supernatural ability, though it was difficult for him to ascertain what that was. After all, he was not familiar with shifters like Cate, with vampires like Lilith, or with hybrids like Orion.

Though he was familiar with fire, it seemed his captors had not fireproofed the place, no doubt an oversight; but an oversight that worked in his favor.

For bit by bit, day by day, Hades had managed to burn through the covered grate beneath the shoddy rug that covered the weathered floors, and no one had been the wiser.

The days were long and cold in the box and had given Hades much to think about. He'd thought of Orion and Trinity, wondered if they had succeeded in their quest, hoping they did; for if not, his long-standing sentence would be in vain and he'd be sitting in a box for nothing.

He'd thought about Cate and Gunner,

about Meg and whether or not she'd finished her book and if she liked the poor sap who was likely sitting at his desk right now, due to his unprecedented absence. He wondered if the stand-in was fucking up his paperwork, putting wet rings on the desk without a coaster.

But most of all, he thought of Darcy.

He'd slide his hands in his pocket, feeling the moonstone he'd taken from the Archives warm in the palm of his hand. When he touched it, he could feel its serenity leaching out to him, as if connecting to him. Providing comfort, relief. Letting him know that somehow, someway, he would see the surface again, and when he did...

The first thing he planned to do was find Darcy Little, and he would never let her go.

Though such daydreams were dramatic, even for Hades, he held on to them.

He longed to see her sparkling blue eyes, kiss her luscious strawberry lips, run his hands through her silky hair and along her flesh.

And, as if the thought alone could materialize her, Hades was pulled from his wandering daydreams due to a large crashing sound outside his door. His flames caught from the instant panic, ready to ignite should the moment diverge into something suitable for defense.

Only it was not Darcy who stood in the doorway. Instead, it was a tall, dark-haired individual with a silver streak and dual-toned eyes who was donning a smirk, and with blue lines of magic surrounding her fingertips.

"Cate? What the hell are you doing here?" Hades asked in confusion, stilling his flames.

"Saving your ass, what does it look like?" she said, rolling her eyes. "Wards are down, but they won't be for long, my magic isn't as strong against the angels anymore," she said in a huff as she looked between Hades and... Lucifer?

Hades crossed his arms just as Lucifer appeared next to her.

"Well, if this sight doesn't prove Hell has frozen over, I'm not sure what does," Hades said with a smirk.

Lucifer stared at him stone-faced as Hades made his way over to them.

"Oh, I can not take all the credit," Lucifer said with a smile.

HADES

Hades's smirk fell, the Diviner against his palm hotter than ever. For the short, slender body that came running, pushing through the fallen angel and goddess was quite the sight for sore eyes.

"I knew it! I knew there had to be an explanation for—"

Darcy's words were cut off in an instant as Hades was before her, wrapping his arms around her waist and lifting her off the ground. Darcy wrapped her legs around his waist, her arms around his neck, and he did not waste any time as he claimed her lips.

A soft squeak escaped her throat, but she relaxed in his hold, her lips burning against his with equal desire and need, and it took all of Hades's concentration to remember they were with an audience.

"Ahem…" Lucifer's clearing his throat pulled Hades back to the here and now. Darcy slid down his front, and the motion stirred his cock, but he pushed it aside for the moment, his eyes falling on Cate and Lucifer.

"How did you find me?" he asked, befuddled.

"Darcy told me… about the two of you. About the Diviner," Cate said softly.

Hades swallowed nervously, but he did not let go of Darcy as he pulled her close, his fingers tightening their grip around her waist. He did not want to let go for fear she'd disappear, evaporate into the cold air of this hellhole like some grand illusion.

"She said she could feel your connection, could feel something was wrong."

Lucifer smirked. "Cate called me, naturally. Never mind that I'd been looking into your disappearance, but for some reason, the footage from the Archives the day you'd been cleared for had gone missing, leaving me and my team of investigators with no leads" Lucifer slid his hands in his pockets and let out a chuckle.

"So, I did some looking on my own, and I found some very interesting items had gone missing. A Diviner, and... an angel tablet. I know you have no use for an angel tablet, especially one warded by your favorite angel, Cassiel."

Hades opened his mouth, but Lucifer held up a hand.

"I don't want to know, Hades. I require plausible deniability. That tablet was not supposed to be in Hell's Archives to begin with, so as far as I am concerned I am glad the cursed thing is gone."

"You knew it was there..." Hades could not hide his shock.

"Of course I knew it was there. I know everything that goes on in my domain. But as you know, the minute anyone touches the thing, Cassiel shows up all dark and brooding and, quite frankly, I can't stand the angel, so I let it fester and collect dust... knowing no one knew it was there..." Lucifer twisted his lips in amusement.

"As far as I am concerned, you did me a service. Consider this a returned favor." Lucifer smiled at Cate. "When Cate called me, claiming Darcy could feel your distress through your... bond... I had a hunch you'd be here."

"I didn't want to believe he was right, but... when Darcy started to tell us that feeling was strong, getting stronger the closer we got to the mountains, I had to admit that maybe..."

"Say it, Cate." Lucifer smirked.

"Maybe, he was right," Cate grumbled.

"Ah yes. Those words make this trip entirely worth it," Lucifer said with a smug look on his face. "However, we don't have much time before Cassiel shows up to find his lackey dead as a doornail, and his wards being broken would likely have already alerted him. So if you wish to get out of this—" Lucifer frowned as he motioned around the room. "Whatever this is, then I suggest you apparate, immediately."

Hades did not waste another moment as

he looked between his friends.

"Thank you," he said as he closed himself around Darcy, and within seconds, they were gone.

CHAPTER TWENTY-SIX

DARCY HELD ON tightly to Hades, the wind rustling her hair and causing goosebumps to erupt on her skin. In a literal flash, she could feel as if they'd moved, her body adjusting to the difference. She kept her eyes closed, the feel of her fingers against his suit jacket, the scent of a warm, cozy fire mixed with his natural scent was practically intoxicating, and Darcy did not want to move, did not want to dislodge herself from the only thing that had stilled the ever present ache in her chest that had been there since the moment he left.

When she opened her eyes, she could see they were in the forest. As she glanced around, she could see an upscale cabin in the distance, sitting atop a hill, the entire front of the house bearing floor to second-story windows that showcased everything.

"Where are we?" she asked in awe.

"Apparently, Cassiel favors hiding out in the hills, but, thankfully, he doesn't own them. There are plenty of retreats and resorts up this way..."

Hades looked down at Darcy, a soft smile tugging at the corners of his mouth.

"I wanted to tell you but I... I had no way. It all kind of happened very quickly, and—" Darcy did not wait as she pulled Hades to her, kissing him with every ounce of forgiveness she had in her being.

"I thought maybe... maybe you changed your mind, but my heart... My heart knew otherwise. Though, I have to admit, the disparity between my heart and my brain made me feel like I was going crazy." She let out a light laugh, and Hades ran his fingers through her hair, down her neck, to her arms. Finally, they stopped at her hand, his fingers intertwining with hers.

"I thought about you every day while I was stuck there, you know," he said as he pulled her toward the path leading up to the glass house, a sexy smile on his face.

"Well, I sure as hell hope so," she

answered with a smile as she let him pull her, leading her.

The walk through the surrounding forest was somehow both relaxing and also alarming. Darcy had never been in woods such as these, and all the little sounds, the chill of the air was making her head spin. Every squeak or snap made her worry, afraid some creature of darkness would show up to invade this perfect fairytale moment where her prince was escorting her to his castle.

When Hades stopped, stone cold still, she had to wonder if she'd been right. He let go of her hand only for a moment as he kneeled down in the dirt, picking up what looked like an antique locket. Darcy noted as he stood, his shoulders tensed, his body straightening as if he'd been touched by lightning.

"Hades..." Darcy said, feeling a pang of worry lace through her.

"Darcy, get behind me." His voice had taken on a serious tone.

"What's wrong, I—"

"Get behind me, now." His voice rose only slightly, but Darcy could hear the urgency in it, and she did as she was told without question.

Hades pulled her close, his grip on her tight and possessive. The locket bristled against her back, the sound tinkling in her ear.

Something about it made her feel quite uneasy.

"What's wrong?" she asked again.

"I can sense death is near..." he said darkly. "But this... this feels different. It feels—" Hades looked down at Darcy with a look that she could only describe as lost.

Empty.

"Close your eyes, darling," he whispered, and Darcy pursed her lips, readying for another jump. Their romantic reunion would have to wait, it seemed.

CHAPTER TWENTY-SEVEN

HADES COULD FEEL his blood run cold as his shoe brushed the antique locket. Though he hadn't seen it in centuries, it did not matter. He knew its presence anyway, and away from its owner was a sign of utter danger. He'd given his former love the only thing he could given the fact she'd forget him.

HADES

He gave her a locket full of memories. A locket that one day she'd open and remember who she was. A force to be reckoned with. A goddess in her own right, she would know all she'd endured, all that she'd overcome, and rise above it all once again.

The way the little golden pocket watch lay in the moist earth, forgotten like a relic, coupled with the stench of panic and fear and the undeniable air of death told Hades two things—Persephone was near, and she was in trouble.

Fresh off the heels of his own rescue, Hades was not certain he was equipped for a rescue of his own, but he would not ignore such a thing, even if it were not his former lover. He could not turn away from a mortal in need, or a mortal on their proverbial deathbed.

So, when Hades wrapped his arms around Darcy, he focused on the scent of death, the vibrations of heightened fear, anxiety, and pain.

When Hades and Darcy appeared deep in the woods, the sight before them was quite unsettling.

Darcy let out a started gasp, followed by an *oh fuck*.

"Hades, is that a..."

"Dragon, darling. Yes. It is," Hades said calmly as his eyes roved over a large beast in front of them with crimson-hued scales and razor-sharp teeth that could surely cut through steel. Hades's gaze scoured down to the beast's gigantic talons, his flames igniting the moment he saw her.

Annabelle lay in the space between the

dragon's talon, her eyes wide with panic as she looked around her, trying to move.

It was almost as if she was spelled to remain in place, as if, somehow, the dragon itself was controlling her movement. Hades could feel the magic all around them, but the sight of her like that, cursed somehow by the aura of this monstrous beast... brought back so many memories.

Ones he thought he'd stuffed down into the pits of Hell itself.

The sound of her labored breaths, her cries echoing in the smoke.

The sight of her hand wrapped around her throat as she gasped for breath, crying out for him.

How her arms held onto him tightly as he ferried her to the surface, the feel of the pain in his chest as she looked up at him with so much love he'd almost turned back.

Hades turned his gaze from the scene before him, settling his hands on Darcy's arms, his grip tighter than he intended.

"I need you to do something for me, darling," he said calmly.

"Wha–what—" Darcy's voice quivered, her eyes still locked on the towering dragon.

Hades let go of her right arm, his fingers gently turning her gaze back toward him. Her bright blue eyes caught his and in them, Hades found the strength he needed to do what he knew he must do.

"I will distract the dragon, and when I do... I need you to watch over—" Hades stopped, unsure of what to say. Surely, with the sight of the opened locket,

HADES

Annabelle had regained her memories. Surely, she knew she was Persephone herself, but yet...

Hades knew it was not as simple as that. This reincarnation, this current being was Annabelle. They were the same person, looked the same, sounded the same but...

The woman in between the dragon's talons was not the woman he'd known.

"I need you to watch over Annabelle."

Darcy's eyes searched his, and it looked as if she wanted to say something, question him even; she herself knew now was not the time for questions. And as soon as the look of curiosity and concern laced her face, it was gone, replaced by a stern look as Darcy pursed her lips and nodded in agreement.

"Okay," she said quietly.

Hades ran his hand through her dark hair, his lips turning up in the corner.

"Good girl. Now, do you see those trees over there?" He nodded to their left, Darcy following his gaze without question.

"Yeah?"

"I want you to take Annabelle on my signal." Hades leaned closer to Darcy, his lips brushing her ear.

"How will I know your signal?" she asked in a hushed tone, even though there was no one around but them, save for the trees and the dragon in front of them.

"Oh trust me, darling. You will know," Hades said as he kissed the soft flesh just underneath her ear, above the pulsing vein in her neck.

"You better not let me die," she said with a dark chuckle.

"You have my word," he whispered. Hades nodded once more to the forest. "Go. Now. Run," he directed her, and Darcy complied.

Hades turned around, running his hands over his suit jacket, straightening his stance. It had been quite a long time since he'd had to channel his power. He'd pushed aside such things, not wanting to feel powerless as he had the day he'd let go of the only woman he ever loved.

But as Hades watched Darcy run for the trees, as he watched her get into position behind the unaware dragon and his prisoner, he knew without a doubt such pain had led him to her.

To his soulmate.

The knowledge alone lit him with a power that struck all throughout him; in his blood, on the surface of his skin and clothes; a fire in his eyes.

Hades stepped out of the clearing as he thrust his arms down at his sides, calling the power within him, and the power from the Earth beneath his feet.

"Hey!" he hollered, his voice larger than he'd remembered when he last used his god voice. The sound echoed off the mountains, ominous and threatening in a way only a vengeful, legendary god could be.

The dragon turned its head, its bright, glowing ruby eyes settling on him with interest. Its forked tongue darted out, licking its spindly teeth, and Hades knew he had his moment.

"Let her go," he ordered. The dragon blew out a breath of fire as Hades sauntered closer.

A rustling in the trees nearby drew his attention, but he did not shift his gaze from the lumbering monstrosity in front of him. Out of his peripheral vision, he could see a distressed man, tall, with dark hair and looking fresh from the fire himself.

"Cade, don't!" Annabelle's voice shrieked, and Hades could feel his flames flickering from the cry of pain, the cry of despair.

"Where are you? " Persephone cried, the fear in her voice evident. "I can't see you... I..."

The deep, guttural coughs stopped her words for too long, and he ran as fast as he could through the smoke. He needed to find her, needed to comfort her.

To save her.

Hades shook the memory from his brain, glancing at the man, Cade, and his disheveled, battered appearance. In his eyes, he saw a look he knew all too well. For Cade's eyes had zeroed in not on the dragon, but on the woman between the talons.

Annabelle.

Of course, he is in love with her.

How could he not be?

A startling feeling ran through Hades at the realization, but it was not jealousy or anger.

It was a relief.

He pulled his gaze from Cade, from Annabelle. Darcy who was now in position and his power felt warm and full, ready to escape once more, ready to be freed.

"We can do this the easy way or the

hard way." Hades looked up at the dragon, and in its shimmering scales, he could see the reflection of his own burning flames.

The ground started to shake as the dragon opened its mouth, letting out a loud, horrific roar before its tail hit him in the waist, sharp like a knife. The pointed scale cut through his suit jacket, his shirt, like butter, and the pain stung like a thousand bees stinging his body. He could feel the blood rushing to the surface, but he did not move to hold his wound, did not tear his eyes away from the brutal force in front of him.

"Fine, the hard way it is," Hades said as he dropped his suit jacket to the ground. He pulled back his arms, letting flames engulf him and the ground started to shake violently, cracks seeming to form from where he stood, seeping out from beneath him and reaching toward the dragon.

Hades cast a large blast of blue fire directly at the dragon, and he screamed as loud as he could, hoping Darcy could hear him amidst the chaos. "Now!"

The world disrupted in red and blue flames, the Earth quaking around them, echoing between the mountains, trees splitting in half from the force. The dragon lunged for him, but he evaded with surprising agility, a dark laugh leaving his throat. It felt good to be powerful again, good to think on his feet, and for the first time since that fateful day, in the eyes of a dragon, Hades found what he thought he'd lost.

Himself.

CHAPTER TWENTY-EIGHT

IT ALL HAPPENED rather quickly, so quickly, in fact, that Darcy was certain she'd never run as fast to retrieve anything as she had at that moment. Hades released a bright blast of blue flame at a dragon that she was certain would haunt her dreams for years to come.

Its red, beady eyes, long scary teeth...

Even its thick scaled body was truly the stuff of nightmares.

But as much as Darcy was frightened, something in the sight of Hades, the way he wielded his power at the creature—gave her hope, gave her courage. Since meeting the god, he'd never asked her for anything. Never pushed her, never led her astray into darker waters where she had to question anything or feel uncomfortable. He'd never asked her for anything until that moment, and she knew she would not let him down.

And so, Darcy sped as quickly as she could, closing her eyes as she skidded on the ground between the legs of a dragon and grabbed onto the woman with dear life. The woman—Annabelle—as Hades had called her, latched onto Darcy.

"Who—" she tried to speak, but Darcy

cut her off.

"I'm here to help," she said with more clarity and confidence than she felt she possessed. The ground shook beneath them, and Darcy tightened her grip on Annabelle. She looked below them, noting the cracks in the Earth and her gaze followed them to their epicenter.

Darcy's gaze traveled the path of blue flame, up long, tapered legs in black slacks, to exposed forearms that jutted out from tight, rolled up shirtsleeves, noting the bright red stain against his hip spreading like ink from an exploded pen. She let her gaze travel up his neck, settling on his eyes of fire, which were glowing so brightly, Darcy would have thought they were stars in the night sky.

Hades stood in the center of the forest,

lit up with electric blue flames all around him, the Earth quaking beneath his feet, his lips pulled back in a smirk as he blasted the dragon, catching his interest like a goldfish catching the cat's. And within a flash, the talons were lifting, the ground shaking, sending vibrations up through her body as Hades ran into the forest, the dragon chasing after him.

Darcy blinked, trying to get her bearings. A part of her could not believe what she saw and she was in shock from the sight. Though she'd had difficulty seeing Hades as the god Cate had described, the evidence was irrefutable in that moment.

He glowed.

He called fire and Earth, and he was every bit a fucking god.

The sight was both highly arousing, and also frightening given the context of the reason he'd channeled the power to begin with.

Darcy shook her head, dispelling the thoughts for the moment. She'd told Hades she would keep watch over Annabelle, and she needed to do that.

"Can you stand?" Darcy asked as she rose, pulling Annabelle with her.

"I... I think so..." Annabelle said as she tried to regain her words.

Darcy could see the alarm in her eyes. Suddenly, another body was entering their private space, and Darcy's grip on Annabelle tightened, her senses on high alert.

"It's okay, I'm—"

"Cade!" Annabelle cried as the man

threw his arms around her.

Darcy's muscles loosened a fraction. At least they know each other, so that's probably a good thing.

"Oh... I swear I wanted to tell you, I just didn't have time. The locket opened, and then all my memories of being Persephone, of Hades... they all came back and—"

Darcy's fingers tightened around Annabelle's arm. "Did you say... Persephone?" she asked shakily.

Cade ran his hands through Annabelle's silvery hair, pulling her close. Annabelle looked up at Darcy with curiosity.

"Yes... and... you were with Hades... You are—"

"Darcy..." Darcy found her throat was tight and words were difficult. If this was truly the same Persephone, the one the legends were written about…

The one who Hades had let go…

Darcy wasn't sure what to say or how to feel. But as she watched Cade and Annabelle, she was certain that whatever had existed once between her and Hades, it was clear it was no longer present in her eyes.

Hades's, however…

Darcy's gaze followed the cracks in the ground, and in the distance, she could see the dragon and the god of the underworld fighting with bright, blinding light, the sounds of roars and deep rumblings echoing in the mountains.

And as soon as she laid eyes on the man with the blue flames, the Earth shook again. Trees rattled, rocks from the mountaintops crumbling down like a landslide as a blast of blue flame engulfed the dragon, who reared its head with a loud roar.

A dying howl.

Darcy, Annabelle, and Cade watched as the dragon erupted into flames, watched as the blue flames licked at the scales, turning them from crimson apples to burned, charred black crisps. The stench of burning flesh reeked through the air like leather and sulfur.

The scent was so strong and overpowering it made Darcy's eyes water, made her feel as if she could gag. She held her hand over her mouth, closing her eyes for only a moment to try and dispel the gruesome sounds and sights, and suddenly, the smell of sulfur and leather dissipated into something much more masculine, and much more pleasing.

"Hades..." she said with relief, her voice on the edge of tears.

"Are you okay?" he asked softly, running his hands through her hair.

Darcy nodded against his chest, a light chuckle of joy escaping her throat as she fought back tears.

"Yes, sir. Very fucking green," she said as she buried her face into his shirt, her hands circling his waist. A warm, wet, sticky liquid smeared along her arm, pulling her back from her thoughts. She held her arm in front of her, noting the smear of blood.

His blood.

"Annabelle, Cade are you—"

"I think I'm okay... I can move... so that's a start," Annabelle said. "Now that the magic has worn off."

Darcy looked up at Hades and noted his eyes were still hazy with a sapphire glow. The sight far away was one thing, but up close... Darcy was in awe.

"You're bleeding," she said.

"It's just a flesh wound, darling. Nothing a little gauze can not fix." He smiled.

Cade and Annabelle were at their side in a flash, and Darcy looked between the two of them. She noted how Cade held Annabelle tightly, as if he were afraid to let go of her, afraid to let her out of his sight.

"Hades... I—" Annabelle sighed, leaning her head against Cade's shoulder.

"I know," he said softly.

"Thank you," she said with tears welling up in her eyes.

"No, thank you," Hades said as he

gripped Darcy tightly.

"I'm glad you got here first," Cade said as he extended his hand to Hades, who took it. "And I'm glad you were here, too." Cade looked at Darcy.

"The two of you helped save Annabelle's life, and I... We can't thank you enough. We are in your debt," Cade said as he shook Hades's hand firmly.

"I believe, actually," Hades spoke as he turned his gaze to Annabelle. "I believe, this makes us even now."

Darcy watched the smile on his face, and somehow in that one glance, it seemed like a weight had fallen off his shoulders.

Annabelle let out a small laugh.

"Well, you'll at least have to let me get you a drink on the house or something," she said with a wink that made Hades blush.

"Ah, yes, the Den Of Sin. Perhaps another time."

Annabelle shrugged. "Whatever."

The rain started to fall as the clouds came in, washing away the scent of a dragon's death, rinsing away the pain and sorrow of yesterday down through the cracks of the Earth that were somehow already starting to heal as if they'd never been there in the first place.

CHAPTER TWENTY-NINE

HADES WATCHED AS Annabelle leaned against Cade, watched as Cade supported her as they made their way through the forest. The way in which he held her, looked at her—the love between them was quite evident.

A part of Hades's heart flooded with relief.

After all the years he'd spent in mourning, years he'd spent trying to forget, to move on, years he'd spent letting guilt consume him—he knew he had done the right thing. He'd given Persephone the chance to live again, and in front of him, she stood in the form of Annabelle. Vibrant, alive, and with the knowledge of who she was, and that was all he ever wanted for her.

To live.

And suddenly, Hades felt a pang in his heart, a longing he'd never truly felt before.

Not for Annabelle, no.

He wanted what she possessed.

Life.

Mortal life.

As Annabelle and Cade disappeared into the trees, Hades realized that was all he'd ever wanted as well.

To live a happy, fulfilling mortal life.

Darcy slid her arm around his waist, bringing him out of his sudden thoughts.

"You were kind of badass back there," she said as she looked at him with sparkling blue eyes that made his cock twitch.

"You really think so?" he asked with a laugh.

"I mean, the blood is a little much, but when you, like, lit up with flames and fucking attacked that monster—" She whistled. "I mean damn. I don't think I've ever seen anything quite that awesome or hot in my life," she said with a blush.

"Well, I am glad you enjoyed my display of—"

"Hotness," Darcy said with a chuckle,

and Hades could not help but smile.

"Sure, we'll go with that."

"You loved her, didn't you?" Darcy asked as they started to walk away from the dragon carcass disintegrating into the ground, away from the battlefield.

"What?" Hades tensed but Darcy did not relent from her grip.

"Persephone," Darcy said the name like a whisper in the wind.

Delicately.

Hades closed his eyes and let out a deep sigh.

"Yes. Once upon a time. A very long time ago," he answered her honestly.

It seemed like an eternity until Darcy spoke, just as they came to the driveway of the house with the glass windows.

"And now?" Her words were so quiet he

could barely hear her.

Hades stopped at the foot of the driveway, looking at her once more. Taking in the sight of her crystalline eyes, her luscious pink lips, how her dark hair fell over her shoulder just so.

He'd spent so many years in solitude afraid. Afraid of falling in love, afraid of opening himself up again to someone like he had with Persephone. But as Hades looked at Darcy against the setting sun of the mountains, he could not deny that he felt more alive with her than he'd ever felt in his long, immortal life. His heart did not yearn for yesterday anymore, it yearned for the promise of tomorrow. It yearned for Darcy Little, front desk attendant at New Haven Animal Rescue.

They stood on the threshold of the glass

house, and Hades smiled before turning from her to unlock the door. He opened it and waited for her to enter.

"Now, I have finally found the person I was truly meant for," he said as Darcy stood only a breath away.

"How did you unlock the house?" She narrowed her eyes at him and he could not help the chuckle that escaped as she fiercely stared him down.

"Darling, I have properties everywhere, but not many people know about them. For a reason."

"So all that back and forth about retreats and spas and shit was just a cover up. You had a house in the mountains all along?"

"Well, if it makes you feel any better, I haven't visited the place since the first spa in the area went in back in the sixties." Hades shrugged as Darcy eyed him suspiciously as she walked through the door into the preserved space. It still looked quite sleek in design, almost like a museum exhibit.

"And the safe house just happened to be in the mountains where you had a house?"

"As I said, not many people know about my surface dwellings. Including Cassiel."

Darcy shrugged as he closed the door, looking around the space in awe.

"Do you like it?" he asked as he came up behind her, feeling the need to reach out and pull her to him once more. The desire to run his hands along her body, tighten their hold on her, was strong, but Darcy turned in his grasp, their lips only a fraction apart. Her hands braced themselves against him, fingers brushing against his wound, and he could not help but wince at the sting.

"We should get you fixed up," she said as she moved his shirt aside, her fingers tracing over the slick, blood-soaked skin.

Hades looked down at her, feeling his own awe.

"I'm—"

"Bleeding. You need treatment. Tell me you have at least some form of first aid in this relic?"

"Relic? You're calling my house a relic?"

"I mean, you did say you haven't been here in like fortyish years, soooo..." Darcy said with a giggle.

"The bathroom upstairs," he whispered in her ear, "should have a first aid kit, if that makes you feel better," he said.

Darcy nodded animatedly. "Mhmmm. Yes. No offense, but I'm not exactly the type to be turned on by blood," she said with a blush as she turned away from him, heading for the modular staircase.

"Come, I will show you to the infirmary," he said with a smirk as he wasted no time climbing the stairs, Darcy not far behind him.

CHAPTER THIRTY

DARCY GINGERLY APPLIED the bandage to Hades's wound. She'd never been the best with blood, the sight of it alone made her weak in the knees, made her feel lightheaded. Though Hades had assured her he was fine, it didn't sit right with her to let it go.

Upon removing his stained shirt, the

sight of his golden skin, his defined muscles, made her entire body flush with heat and she had to concentrate heavily on her task, lest she turn into a puddle of desire on his black marble bedroom floor.

Hades tried his best to appear unphased, but the moment Darcy had dabbed the alcohol soaked cotton ball against his wound, he hissed, wincing, even if only slightly.

"Ah, so you do feel pain," Darcy said with a smirk.

"Of course I feel pain," Hades said as he leaned back against the headboard, his eyes rolling up toward the ceiling, a deep sigh leaving his chest.

Darcy swiftly ripped open the bandage package, taking her time as she applied the antibiotic. A part of her felt as if the whole situation was moot, after all, he was a god, he was immortal, incapable of death. But years of being around injured animals, some experience with very physical ex-boyfriends who spent much more time kickboxing and sparring at the gym than was probably necessary, and years of having to tend to her own clumsy wounds from just living in her small and ill-equipped apartment, meant Darcy's skills were more efficient than most when it came to injuries.

Hades lay against the bed, his gaze fixated on the ceiling still, and Darcy could see the rise and fall of his perfect tanned chest as she softly approached his wound, which looked much less bloody now that it had been cleaned, and more like a deep gash.

"What's the worst injury you've ever had?" she asked as she leaned closer to him on the bed, slowly applying the bandage.

Hades did not pull his gaze from the ceiling, clearly focusing on the tiny swirls in the plaster.

"After..." he paused, almost as if he was worried to continue.

Darcy slid her hand over the bandage, smoothing it out, giving him a moment.

"I ferried Persephone to the surface. I was not prepared for the pain it would cause me. I was... in a very dark place."

Darcy did not remove her hand from his bandage, but she watched him, his expressions, the way his body tensed as he remembered his past.

"I was very combative. Looking for a

fight wherever I could, seeking out the pain because, in those moments..."

Hades sighed, his hand sliding over Darcy's as he pulled his gaze from the paint swirls in the ceiling and fixed his dark, beautiful brown eyes on her.

"If I could feel physical pain, I couldn't feel the heartache. It was like I could finally breathe."

Hades's eyes searched hers, but she wasn't certain what it was he was looking for.

Acceptance, understanding?

No, she realized as his hand on top of hers heated, as she fell into his space like a falling star.

She understood in that one moment, the way in which he looked at her exactly what he was searching for.

Permission.

Darcy climbed on the bed, settling next to him as she tucked her legs underneath her, leaning against his trim, defined tanned chest, never moving her hand from beneath his. She looked back into his eyes, and in them, she could see the pain he'd carried for so long, could see the hope and desire for something to eradicate it.

"I've gone through a lot of... scenarios... before I'd stumbled upon the Den Of Sin. Before I met Tenille."

"Tenille is—"

"Was, darling. Tenille *was* my... pain management system." Hades averted his gaze, as if afraid to see judgment waiting for him. It only took a moment for Hades's words to sink in fully.

"She was your... Domme?" Darcy asked

calmly.

Was that the right word?

"I prefer the term mistress, but, yes. She was."

"What happened to her?" she asked nervously, wondering if Tenille, too, had gone the way of Persephone and if Hades himself was some curse. He certainly looked the part, especially in the low light of the bedroom, bandaged, shirtless, with that dark look in his eye, shadows casting about his abs, his dark hair, and slender neck.

"Our agreement was no longer what I wanted, and we parted ways."

A palpable silence lay between them, unspoken words hanging in the air.

"Does it still hurt?" Darcy's voice was soft, unsure of which wound she was truly referring to. She glanced down to their hands upon his bandage, Hades stroking the back of her knuckles with his index finger. The feeling alone, the slow, almost feather light touch causing her blood to heat, causing her heart to flutter.

"Only when I am away from you," he whispered shakily.

Darcy could feel her insides turning, her own heart beating faster at his words, and she could not fight any of it; her feelings, her desires, her dreams. She leaned into him, pulling his face toward her, and into a sweet kiss. Careful not to agitate his fresh wound, she shifted her body against his lightly.

Hades kissed her back, the hunger more than evident in the way he bit at her lower lip before sucking it softly, the way his tongue softly caressed hers as he deepened their kiss. A soft sound escaped his throat and Darcy felt warm from her head to her toes.

She leaned into him, her arms around his neck pulling him closer, but Hades slid his hands down her side, finding their way between the waistband of her jeans and her flesh. His fingernails dug into the skin of her ass and he pulled her forward.

Darcy let out a surprised sound, but followed his pull, straddling his legs, all the while careful not to disturb his fresh bandage.

Hades's hand slid over the flesh of her ass once more, his lips caressing her jaw, her neck.

Her hand cascaded down his chest, settling over his heart. The rhythmic beat underneath her touch stirred a thousand emotions within her.

"Oh, Hades." Her voice thick with desire, hung on his name like a prayer.

"I love it when you call my name," he whispered darkly in her ear as his hands slid up underneath her shirt.

Darcy did not wait as she removed it, breaking away from him only for a moment. She could hear the desire in his voice; sending an echo through her own body at the dark way in which he praised her.

"Yeah?" she asked huskily as she unhooked her bra, letting it fall to the bedding beside them. Her nipples became stiff peaks against the onslaught of chilled air, but the chill was soon met by a warm, wet mouth, a soft tongue that lapped at her sensitive flesh tenderly. Hades's hands rode up her back, pulling her closer, and Darcy felt as if it would never be enough.

It would never be enough until they were one, intertwined together. A wave of confidence overcame her, and though she'd never been the most dominant of personalities, especially when it came to sex—she found that with Hades she longed to be more than what she'd always attributed herself to be. He brought out a side of her she'd never known. A side of her which felt strangely emblazoned by his deep, dark voice, ignited by the blue flicker of flames that surrounded them, giving her life.

"Hades," she moaned louder, noting the pressure of his grip tightening against her.

"Darcy..." he purred, her name most

sinful on his tongue. The sound, the way he rolled his r, the way his voice echoed in the room, was a most pleasant sound to her.

His hands slid down her backside once more to her waistband, circling around to her front, his fingers deftly unbuttoning her jeans, and Darcy met his adamant need with her own.

The chill of the air against their skin, the warmth of their bodies in the space between a most heavenly feeling.

The race against time to tear their clothes off was much quicker than she'd expected; their need for one another a force all its own; driving them.

"What do you want me to do, Sir?" she breathed out huskily, knowing just how much he liked the words. She found that they came naturally, and she didn't mind it, either.

Hades stared up at her for a long moment, his hands frozen against her back.

Darcy freed his cock from his boxers, the last remaining bit of clothing that remained a barrier between them. In Hades's eyes, she could see he was nervous, and she wondered why.

She leaned her body against his, her hand sliding over his pectorals as she looked at him with all the love she had in her body, hoping he understood there was nothing to be scared of here.

In this house, in this bed.

With her.

"I…"

"What? What is it? Are you yellow or—"

Darcy asked, trying to keep the panic out of her voice.

"No, it's not that, it's..." Hades licked his lips as his eyes roved over her naked form like she was Venus de Milo.

"You are so unbelievably fucking beautiful." He sighed as he pulled her lips to his, kissing her softly. She could feel the tremble in them, though, like the Earth feels tremors right before a giant tsunami overtakes the land. "I need to know where you are first," he said as he leaned his forehead against hers.

Her fingers lightly traced his jaw.

"Very fucking green, Hades," she said. "You?"

"Green light, darling," he breathed out. His gaze caught hers and she could feel the weight of the unspoken words between them.

"I want to please you, Darcy..." The way he said the words... it was simple, yet, the trust, and the emotion in them was not lost.

The last time they'd been here, like this, was months ago, and it had all been a heated blur. Everything had moved at the speed of light, the way they'd torn their clothes off, the hard and fast way in which he'd grabbed her, fucked her. She could still remember reaching for him, remembered him forcing her against the bed frame.

His words, *I want you to please me.*

And she had, but it wasn't the sex that she thought about in all the months he'd been gone, though those thoughts certainly permeated her psyche enough. It was the way he'd looked at her afterward. The way he reacted to seeing the marks on her skin, how he'd drawn her a bath. How he held her close, curling his body around hers, legs intertwined in the sheets as they drifted off to slumber.

Suddenly, the veil of lust came crashing down around them.

Hades did not break her gaze as his fingers gripped her hips tightly. The raw vulnerability within those words meant more than sex, more than a desire to bring her pleasure.

It was Hades laying his heart out on a silver platter, and trusting that she would love him, that she would accept him as he was, god and all.

Flaws and all.

It was the deepest promise and it came

from the depths of the Earth, the depths of Hades himself, and that kind of vulnerability, that kind of trust...

Who could deny that?

For Darcy loved him for all that he was, and she knew in that moment nothing could ever change that.

"Tell me... tell me what you want me to do. Tell me how to please you," he whispered, swallowing nervously. The words were foreign to him, she realized.

Darcy swallowed, finding her own words, her own breath as she slid forward, rubbing herself against the hardened exterior of his cock between her legs, kissing the spot just below his ear. She took a deep breath, forcing down the stray giggle that threatened to erupt due to nerves. She'd never been the most commanding in the bedroom, but in Hades's arms she was someone else, and so she whispered, "Well, for starters, H, I really, really like it when you take that delicious mouth of yours between my legs and eat my pussy like it's your last meal on the planet."

She watched Hades's eyes dilate at her words, noting how his cock twitched against her, watched as the sexy smile replaced his look of nervousness.

Hades grasped her around the waist before flipping her backward onto the bed, putting himself over top of her as he loomed over her. The force was unexpected but she did not mind.

His lips started at her earlobe, biting it gently before whispering darkly in her ear. "That's because you taste so good, like rivers of milk and honey." He dragged his tongue along her neck as his hands settled on her hips. "And I don't know about you, darling, but I'm fucking starving," he said smoothly, and Darcy watched as his head dipped between her legs, her insides already building with anticipation.

The moment his tongue found her already swollen clit, she let out a strangled moan, her back arching instantly. It was as if all her nerve endings had come alive from the heat, from the feel of his lips alone. It felt just as divine as the first time, and she knew if she let him, he'd drive her over the edge into oblivion far too soon.

"Fucking Hell, Hades..." she moaned, her body feeling flush with heat. Her hands found his head, fingers tangling in his dark hair as she tightened her grip. Within seconds, his tongue plunged into her, his thumb rubbing against her clit in a tortuous rhythm. Darcy's insides started to climb higher and higher, and she had to force the words out against the ecstasy that overtook her.

"I want more, Hades... I want..." Hades slid a finger into her soaked entrance, his lips biting and sucking at her outer folds and the pressure made Darcy's legs tighten around his head.

"M–more..." She shut her eyes, and her breaths started to come faster and she could feel herself on the edge of coming.

Hades pulled his lips from her aching loins and he kissed her flesh all the way up to her breasts, biting and sucking once more before finally finding Darcy's lips again, kissing her, shoving his tongue in her mouth once more.

She could taste the remnants of herself on his tongue, and though she couldn't agree with him that it tasted like milk and honey, it wasn't... terrible. And quite frankly, she didn't mind it as much as she thought she would, now knowing what to expect.

"My darling wants more, hm?" he whispered darkly against her lips.

Darcy nodded.

"Yes," she panted. "I want to feel you, I—" Darcy pushed herself up, and Hades fell back into a sitting position. She looked over his body, taking in the sight of him before her; sun-kissed skin, dark hair, and eyes full of lust, of love. He was breathtaking, and he was hers.

My soulmate.

The words of desire were lost in the air as Darcy leaned closer, pushing Hades into the sheets. He did not break her gaze, and when she had managed to crawl over top of him, she could feel the wetness on the end of his cock as it pressed against her stomach. She could not help the words that came out her mouth next.

"I want all of you, Hades."

CHAPTER THIRTY-ONE

"I WANT ALL of you, Hades."

Darcy's words hit his ears, and the way his entire body reacted was not as he had expected. It flooded with relief, with longing. Hades wanted all of Darcy Little, his soulmate.

"Your wish is my command, darling," he whispered against her ear as he lined himself up beneath her, never breaking her gaze, wanting nothing more than to watch her face as he filled her.

Darcy sank down on top of him, and the warm feeling of being inside her filled him with so much ecstasy he could hardly focus. She felt so good, her insides wrapped around his cock.

Darcy's eyes fluttered, her mouth opening just slightly enough for the sounds to come out that was music to Hades's ears. A wave of desire flooded him, but emotion also bubbled beneath the surface as he braced himself into an upright position. Darcy brought her arms around him, pulling herself closer, flush to his chest, and buried her head against his neck.

It was only five months ago the thought

of her touching him like this threw him into a panic. He'd turned her over, stilling her arms so she couldn't reach him, couldn't access the part of him he was afraid to let anyone near. But now, in this moment, as she wrapped her arms around him, as she clung to his body, thrusting her hips forward, building a rhythm against him, he could not help but close his eyes, wrapping his arms around her and letting the last bit of his armor fall to the ground. He murmured the words he'd never thought he'd speak again.

"I love you," he whispered softly in her ear, thrusting up into her as she bucked her hips forward.

"Oh, Hades..." Darcy moaned as she took his lips against hers. "I love you, too."

The world beneath them shook just

enough that the shelves dispelled their books and knickknacks, but Hades did not care. For his fire ignited like a burning pyre, encasing him and his destined lover in its blessed heat, mixing with the desire and love as the two of them raced toward their pleasure faster and faster, until the world disappeared and for the first time in Hades's long life, he felt free.

Darcy came around him, his name a strangled sound of ecstasy as he filled her with his own release. They both lay intertwined together for what seemed like eternity and Hades knew the answer to the question he had thought about for far too long.

He knew exactly how this could work. How they could work, how they could just... be.

Once they had separated, Darcy curled into his side, throwing her arm over his chest, and he pulled her close, playing with the ends of her hair. He took in the sight of her; her peaceful slumber, the soft rise and fall of her chest. The smell of coconut and vanilla was sweet and alluring all at once.

Soulmate.

That was who Darcy was.

His sun, his moon, and his stars.

He'd given her the one thing he'd held so dear for far too long; power.

Power over him, power to rule him.

She'd embraced this new power willingly, and kindly, and he knew without a doubt, the final straw had broken. He could trust Darcy Little with the very thing that was more valuable to him than power itself.

His soul.

And as the sun came up, shining through the trees of the mountains, falling on Darcy like the angel she truly was, Hades knew that this was the day his life truly began.

CHAPTER THIRTY-TWO

IT WAS A day like any other day in Hell. Although Lucifer had given Hades what he called an "extended leave," Hades knew there was no way he would be returning to the Underworld.

Not now.

Not after all that had happened, and not after what he was about to do.

Hades stood in front of the large door, readying himself to knock, surprised that the door swung open of its own accord to reveal a white-haired woman with captivating eyes and a smirk that could rival even Orion.

"Hades, to what do we owe the pleasure?" Chloe said with much interest. She, of all people, knew he did not make house visits.

"I request an audience with—"

"Who the hell is it?" Lucifer called in the background. Chloe rolled her eyes. "Come on in," she said as she waved him in, yelling back to Lucifer only after the door shut.

"It's Hades!"

Hades suddenly felt nervous. His palms started to sweat and his heartbeat started to quicken and he thought perhaps, for a moment, he was truly out of his mind. Once the tall, devilishly attractive fallen angel made his presence known, staring Hades down with a sly grin, Hades knew there was no escaping.

Not now, not ever.

There was only one way out of Hell for him.

Lucifer nodded in his direction, calling for Hades to follow him. He did so wordlessly. Once they'd reached Lucifer's vast library, he shut the door quietly.

"Well, I'd say I'm happy to see you, but I think we both know you coming here is not a social call, so let's dispense the pleasantries, shall we?" Lucifer said as he motioned for Hades to sit down in a large, baroque style chair. Though typical baroque fashion would have been much more refined and regal. Everything in Lucifer's castle was some mash-up of ancient and modern. Ornate motifs were strewn all throughout the place, but everything was a palette of black and red. Hades never cared for it.

"Very well, then," Hades said as he took a seat, waiting for Lucifer to sit in his giant throne-sized chair behind his onyx desk.

"I will not waste your time with explanations or stories, I just... I would like to have my soul, please."

Hades said the words and they felt strange. He'd gone over the phrase in his head multiple times, but yet, saying the words aloud felt as if he was asking for nothing more than a cup of tea, when in fact, he was asking for the very essence that made him who he was.

Lucifer sighed as he folded his hands in his lap. It was a long moment before he spoke.

"It's not a simple insertion process," Lucifer said calmly.

"I don't want it reinstated. I want to make a deal."

Lucifer cocked his head to the side, an expression of curiosity falling across his face.

"I beg your pardon?"

"I want to make a deal. An ironclad one that not even you can go back on."

Lucifer leaned forward in his chair, his eyes sparkling with interest.

"You know I don't make deals anymore, Hades."

"I think for this you will make an

exception," Hades said as he leaned forward in his chair.

"By all means..." Lucifer gestured to him to continue.

"I want to trade my powers for my soul."

"Your powers? Your godly powers? The very thing that makes you immortal... for your soul?" The shock on Lucifer's face would have been funny if the situation was not quite so serious.

"Why, a soul without your powers would make you..."

"Mortal, yes."

"Have you considered the consequences of what you are asking... thoroughly?"

Hades had thought about it. Plenty of times.

"I have."

"Have you discussed this with your

sisters at all?" Lucifer sat straighter in his chair.

"You know the answer to that. Had I told Demi or Hera about this, I certainly wouldn't be here."

"I don't need them breaking down my door to undo what you've asked, you know."

"It's not like I won't be able to see them ever again," Hades said softly. Even as he said the words, he knew it would be an adjustment. He could still visit Hell occasionally, pop in for a bite at the ButterNut Bakery, or meet up for coffee at the DeLux, but nothing more than twenty-four hours. A human soul wasn't made for the Underworld, and he knew better than anyone what prolonged exposure would do to a mortal body.

"You won't be able to withstand the weather down here," Lucifer said with a smirk.

"It's always been a bit balmy, if you ask me," Hades said with a smirk of his own. "I can come back, just... not as frequently," Hades said the words, feeling a sense of sadness. "Besides. The door goes both ways. You all can travel between realms."

Lucifer let out a sigh. "I've always known this day would come. Although, I didn't know I would feel this way when it did." He looked in Hades's eyes, and reflected in them, Hades could see the beginning of his own sadness starting to emerge.

"I'm going to miss the paperwork being turned in on time," Lucifer said with a chuckle, but Hades knew it was only to cover up his feelings.

The sight made Hades realize he, too, would miss the devil himself.

"I'm not going to miss you chewing out my ass when it wasn't." Hades let out a soft chuckle of his own.

Lucifer opened his drawer and pulled out a long piece of parchment, and a raven's quill.

Hades focused on Lucifer's swift motions, watched as the quill glided across the paper like butter.

They just don't make correspondence like this anymore.

As quickly as he'd scribbled the words down, the paper was in Hades's hands, and Lucifer was up from his chair, sauntering over to the massive wall that was nothing but bookshelves, stopping only to pull a book which Hades noticed was not a book, but a lever.

The door popped open to reveal a steel-lined chamber, and Lucifer paused for a moment, his gaze settling on Hades before he disappeared in the vault. It seemed like hours to Hades until he had resurfaced with a small black box.

Lucifer stood in front of Hades with the box as Hades looked over the parchment once more, knowing that within moments, his life would be his until death came for him.

"I to die and you to live. God only knows which is better," Lucifer said as he held the black box in the palm of his hand.

Hades could not help the smirk on his face as he pulled it from his hand.

"I thought you hated Plato," he said as

he ran his fingers over the velvet box, his heart beating loudly in his chest.

"The man was a pain in the ass, but he was right about a few things," Lucifer said quietly.

"Thank you," Hades said, emotion catching in his throat. He looked up at his friend to see the same emotion on his face, and Lucifer nodded in response.

CHAPTER THIRTY-THREE

IT HAD BEEN barely two weeks since the fiasco in the woods with the dragon, Persephone—no, Annabelle—and Cade. Since Hades had called forth his power, showing her who he truly was. Though according to Hades, he'd been given an extended leave to recuperate from his kidnapping and rescue mission, Hades had gone back to Hell to debrief. A part of her worried that he'd disappear again, but Hades had more than convincing in his bouts to reassure her he would not.

And he'd kept his word. Upon the celebrating ding of a text message during lunch, Darcy felt a sense of relief, of joy.

Pick you up at Taco Tim's at eight?

She'd typed yes so quickly not even autocorrect could salvage her response, but she knew he'd get the message.

So as she ran her fingers through her dark hair, applying one more coat of lipstick, adjusting her cleavage once more, she could not help the excitement coursing through her.

A knock on her door startled her, and she nearly jumped off the ground. Maybe he just couldn't wait, she thought with a smile. Only, to her surprise as she opened the door there was no one there. Darcy looked to her left, then to her right, but there was nothing, no one. She moved to shut the door, figuring it was probably a neighbor kid goofing off, but just as she moved to shut the door she saw it. A post-it note on the floor. She opened the door slightly, kneeling down in her brightly colored dress, balancing on the heels of her rhinestone shoes.

She picked up the post-it. All it said was *DeLux*.

And just as she moved to stand, she saw another one in the hallway. Darcy quickly grabbed her clutch, turning to lock the door as she picked up the next post-it note, which read *Judd's*.

She followed the trail further down to

the stairs, picking up another that read *Taco Tim's*.

One by one, Darcy followed the post-its out to the parking lot of Taco Tim's but she did not see Hades standing there, and so she sat at the picnic table, a stack of post-its in one hand, and her cellphone in the other. She noted the time was eight o'clock sharp.

A honking horn startled her and one of the cars, a rather sleek looking black sports car, flashed its lights at her. She shielded her eyes momentarily, squinting. And when she saw a familiar face leaning out of the window, she couldn't help but smile.

"Maybe I should have put a post-it note on the car?" he said with a laugh, and within seconds, Darcy was up, squealing with excitement as she hurried over to the passenger side, jumping into Hades's car.

The interior was just as sleek and sexy in design as the outside.

"So, finally got an official car for your Lyft gig, huh?"

"You could say that," he said with a smirk as he turned the car on, the engine purring like a kitten.

"I liked the notes," she said with a giggle.

"When I thought about the places I wanted to go the next time I came topside, I realized I'd already found the best places."

He pulled out of the parking lot, speeding off into the hills. "Really, H? I mean, Taco Tim's is top-notch, but Judd's?" Darcy made a concerned face.

"All places I have fond memories of

because I've been there with you."

Darcy could feel her cheeks starting to redden at his words.

"Oh, I... I guess that's one way to look at it," she said sweetly.

Hades reached out his hand and set it on her thigh.

"I hope you are hungry, because tonight, I will share one of my favorite places with you."

"I can't wait," Darcy exclaimed excitedly.

When they pulled up to the bamboo hut, Darcy was more than excited. She'd always wanted to go to the Mermaid Bar, but never ventured out that far. She followed Hades in the compact, tight bar as they both took seats in front of the bar.

"What can I get ya?" the bartender asked with a drawl, and Darcy could tell it was genuinely southern.

"I'll have a Manhattan," Hades said as he looked at Darcy with question. "And my lovely date will have a Summer Slushie."

Darcy felt an instant pang of defiance, and she wanted to protest. She could order her own drink, but then again, she remembered this was noted to be one of his favorite places, so it was likely he knew what was good here better than she would, having never been to the establishment herself.

Soon enough, the bartender served their drinks, and Darcy's eyes widened. The drink was served in a fancy glass with so much fruit it should have been considered part of the food pyramid. But it wasn't the fruit that made her heart skip with joy.

It was the little tiny blue umbrella

sticking out over the side.

"It even has an umbrella," she said with a giggle as she took a sip of the drink. It was sweet, so sweet, in fact, Darcy was certain that two of these things would land her on the floor because she could barely taste the alcohol.

"I know," Hades said with a smile that lit up his eyes. He winked at her and she couldn't help but meet his smile. "The other night—" he started, his shoulders tensing.

Darcy watched his demeanor as it shifted to something a bit more serious.

"What about it?" she asked, taking another sweet sip.

"I had an epiphany, you could say," he said as he swirled the ice in his drink.

"Oh?"

"I have always told Cate that she needed to live in the moment. That the little moments are where life is truly visible, truly lived. Little moments like eating tacos at three in the morning with a beautiful woman, or playing pool in a bar with strangers, or—"

Darcy watched as Hades's cheeks flushed red.

"Or watching a movie in the park..."

"Chucky and chill," Darcy said with a laugh, and Hades shook his head.

"Until I met you, Darcy, I thought I was living. Writing down all the sights on little post-it notes, trying to see what I could of the world in the short holidays I took. But I wasn't living. I was existing. The years flew right by me and I did not even blink. I'd built a life around consistency, around the order. And then... then, I went to the DeLux cafe on a whim, and I was thrown into a series of events that shifted everything, and suddenly, I realized that I've never felt more alive in my entire life than I do when I am with you."

Darcy could feel the weight of his words, and she set her drink down. Hades reached in his pocket, and an alarm shot through her.

He's not...

When he pulled out a small, black box and set it on the counter, her heart stopped. He pushed it gently toward her.

"Hades..." she whispered, suddenly out of breath.

"Open it." His voice was clear, not commanding or authoritative, but... real.

Darcy could feel her heartbeat in every

part of her body, and she was certain the rest of the world could feel it, hear it, too.

She picked up the lightweight box, her fingers trembling as she pushed it open. Set in black velvet was a teardrop sapphire set against the brightest silver, surrounded by an outline of black diamonds. The gem glittered in the low light of the bar, its facets catching on the light. But the part that was most beautiful was the shimmering center that looked as if the light was trapped within. It danced like blue smoke in the tiny gem, changing color and shape at every angle, like flames flickering and changing shape against the wood it burns.

"Oh, Hades, it's..."

"My soul," he said as he took a long drink of his Manhattan, signaling the bartender for another. He ran his hand through his hair.

Darcy looked up at him with surprise.

"What?"

"After I ferried Persephone to the surface, after I fell into that dark, dark place... I asked Lucifer to take my soul. I thought it would be the answer, that by losing the part of me that made me human... I thought it would take away the pain, the grief. I didn't want to feel those things." Hades pulled the gem from the box, and Darcy could see it was a ring. Set in the brightest silver, its blue hue the color of the flames she'd seen on him so many times. Hades took her hand softly, sliding the dainty ring on her finger, and Darcy felt as if she would expire on the spot.

ARIEL DAWN

This can't be real, I must be dreaming, I...

Darcy ran her finger over the smooth, cut sapphire surface, appreciating the beauty of the first soul she'd ever seen, and her eyes filled with tears as understanding washed over her, as his words fell on her ears.

"I thought the answer was to split my existence. That keeping Persephone in Hell six months out of the year was the right thing to do, but it wasn't. Mortals were never built to withstand the world as we were. But it wasn't until I saw her with Cade that I understood. I'd rather spend the rest of my days numbered, if they're numbered with you. I'd rather live today with you, Darcy, than live a hundred lives where you don't exist. I want to live."

Darcy felt the tears come to her eyes and she finally looked up at Hades.

"I promise to keep it safe," she said shakily.

Hades set his hand on her knee, a smile crossing his lips.

"I know you will." Darcy closed the box, holding it against her heart as she leaned into Hades's space and kissed his lips with a silent promise. "You have bewitched me, body and soul, and I love, love, love you. I never wish to be parted from you, from this day on, Darcy," he whispered against her lips.

Darcy let out a little laugh as she broke away, looking up into his beautiful brown eyes.

"Did you just quote fucking Pride and Prejudice to me?"

Hades's eyes turned up in the corners as he smiled.

"You actually read that?"

"I mean, like everyone's read that. It's like, required reading for high schoolers," she said as the tears fell from her eyes, wiping them as she laughed.

"Well Hell, I thought I was being smooth, but clearly I've been exposed," Hades said, rolling his eyes as he brought his freshly refilled Manhattan to his lips.

Darcy reached her hand out, tangling her fingers with his.

"One cannot be always laughing at a man without now and then stumbling on something witty," she said with a wink.

Hades drained the last of his drink and pushed it toward the bartender.

"Touché, Miss Little," he said with a

smile as Darcy swiveled away from him once more, biting off the cherry on the end of her umbrella toothpick, savoring the taste for as long as it lasted on the tip of her tongue.

And when Hades walked her up the stairs, unable to apparate any longer, she did not think twice about kissing him, did not think twice about asking him to stay.

When the sun came up the next day, lighting up the insides of Darcy's apartment, it caught on a bright blue gem, refracting in beams all around the room. And as Hades pulled Darcy close, she felt as if she could live forever, and when they kissed in the morning light, that is exactly what they did.

Thank you for reading!

Follow our Facebook page here: <u>Speed Dating with the Denizens of the Underworld Series</u>

Watch your favorite online retailer for the other books in the Speed Dating with the Denizens of the Underworld series.

Turn the page now for an excerpt from Lilith by Carrie Pulkinen, Book Fifteen in the Speed Dating with the Denizens of the Underworld series!

EXCERPT

**Has the world's first vampire found a
match made in hell?**

"BITE ME," HE whispered against her lips.

She sucked in a sharp breath and
pulled back to look into his eyes. "Are you
sure?"

His grip tightened on her hip. "No

glamour. I want to feel everything."

"Have you ever been bitten?" Her voice was breathless.

"No, not that I'm aware of."

She let out a slow exhale as if relishing the idea of being his first. "Let's go inside. If your feelings for me are remotely close to mine for you, my bite will lead to other things...things I would rather do in private."

Sweet Lucifer's testicles, this woman was hot. Her curves fit perfectly against his frame, and her luscious minty, floral scent made his head spin. She might have been a siren leading him to his death, but at this moment, it didn't matter. He would take pleasure in his demise.

Snag Lilith by Carrie Pulkinen now at your favorite online retailer!

Watch for the other books in the

Speed Dating with the Denizens of the

Underworld Series

<u>Lucifer</u>

<u>Ash</u>

<u>Azrael</u>

<u>Samael</u>

<u>Azazel</u>

<u>Hecate</u>

<u>Bastet</u>

<u>Cain</u>

<u>Thor</u>

<u>Demi</u>

<u>Hell's Belle</u>

<u>Arachne</u>

<u>Osiris</u>

<u>Hades</u>

Lilith

HADES

Adam

Loki

Orion

Hera

Abel

Odin

Zeus

Michael

Asterion

Apollo

Raphael

Baldur

Poseidon

Gabrielle

Seth

Athena

Triton

Medusa

And More!

OTHER BOOKS BY ARIEL DAWN

Speed Dating with the Denizens of the Underworld Series

Hecate

Hades

Orion

The Forevermore Series

In The Cards

In The Blood

HADES

In The Shadows

In The Deep

In The Garden

In The Night-coming soon!

Shifters Of Starfall Creek Series

Hollow's Sunrise

Hollow's Sunset

Hollow's Legacy

Shifters of Starfall Creek Collection:

Books 1-3

Get a copy of Ariel Dawn's short story, Faded, when you sign up for her newsletter!

https://mailchi.mp/e5f326e433bf/dawn -breaks-official-newsletter

CONNECT WITH ARIEL DAWN

Website

http://www.ariel-dawn.com

Goodreads:

http://www.goodreads.com/authorarieldawn

Bookbub:

http://www.bookbub.com/authors/ariel-dawn

Facebook:

http://www.facebook.com/authorarieldawn

Twitter:

https://twitter.com/ArielDawn10

Join Dusk Chasers—Ariel Dawn's Official Readers Group for access to exclusive content!

ABOUT ARIEL DAWN

USA TODAY BESTSELLING AUTHOR Ariel Dawn grew up as an avid reader and is a creative soul.

What started out as writing reviews for indie romance authors led to featuring quirky, stereotypical, and weird covers on her Instagram Wrong Turn Romance, which gave her the courage to finally decide to live her dream and become an author.

Ariel writes plot driven paranormal romance and hopes to venture into fantasy and rom-com in the future. When she isn't writing, she can be found cosplaying, attending conventions, creating all sorts of artwork in her studio, or editing photos for her photography business.

A self-professed geek and foodie, she loves hanging out with family and friends and playing video games and board games with her retro gamer husband.

www.ingramcontent.com/pod-product-compliance
Lightning Source LLC
Chambersburg PA
CBHW061047210726
48294CB00001B/47